COCKTAILS AND CRIME

An Anthology

of the Lighter Side

of Francis Durbridge

Francis Durbridge

WILLIAMS & WHITING

Cover design by Timo Schroeder

9781915887047

Williams & Whiting (Publishers)
15 Chestnut Grove, Hurstpierpoint,
West Sussex, BN6 9SS

Titles by Francis Durbridge published by Williams & Whiting

Murder At The Weekend – the rediscovered newspaper serials and short stories

Also published by Williams & Whiting:
Francis Durbridge : The Complete Guide
By Melvyn Barnes

Titles by Francis Durbridge to be published by Williams & Whiting

Murder On The Continent (Further re-discovered serials and stories)
News of Paul Temple
One Man To Another – a novel
Operation Diplomat
Paul Temple and the Alex Affair
Paul Temple and the Canterbury Case (film script)
Paul Temple and the Conrad Case
Paul Temple and the Geneva Mystery
Paul Temple and the Lawrence Affair
Paul Temple and the Margo Mystery
Paul Temple: Two Plays For Radio Vol 2 (Send For Paul Temple and News of Paul Temple)
The Passenger
Tim Frazer and the Salinger Affair
Tim Frazer and the Melynfforrest Mystery

INTRODUCTION

Francis Durbridge (1912-98) began his career in 1933 as a writer for BBC radio. Many of his scripts were intended for children, others were light plays or musical comedies, but soon a talent for crime fiction became evident in his radio plays *Murder in the Midlands* (1934) and *Murder in the Embassy* (1937).

In 1938 Durbridge introduced his most durable creation, the dream team of novelist/detective Paul Temple and his wife Steve. The serial *Send for Paul Temple* proved an instant success, and led to many sequels until 1968 that gave Durbridge an impressive UK and European fanbase. He remained a mainstay of BBC radio for many years, writing under his own name and also using the pseudonyms Frank Cromwell, Nicholas Vane and Lewis Middleton Harvey. Then in 1952, while continuing to write for radio, he embarked on a long run of BBC television serials that attracted huge viewing figures until 1980. And additionally, from 1971 in the UK and even earlier in Germany, he became known for intriguing stage plays that were not simple whodunits but more in the style of Frederick Knott, Ira Levin or Anthony Shaffer.

Crime fiction devotees will associate Durbridge primarily with the radio exploits of Paul Temple, television thrillers such as *The Scarf, The World of Tim Frazer* and *Melissa*, and numerous novelisations of his radio and television serials. But long forgotten are most of his early radio works because few recordings have survived, which makes the recent discovery of some of his 1930s and 1940s typescripts extremely significant and provides the opportunity to publish them. So this volume presents fourteen lighthearted Durbridge scripts that were broadcast between 1935 and 1941.

Stranger, Beware, broadcast on 18 April 1941, is a forty minute musical comedy – but Durbridge, ever the consummate recycler, had already used the main plot idea just a few months earlier in an episode of the non-musical *And Anthony Sherwood Laughed*. *The House on the Corner*, broadcast on 24 December 1941, is a forty-five minute musical play – and Durbridge later re-used the central idea as a sub-plot in his serial *Farewell, Leicester Square* (1943) under the pseudonym Lewis Middleton Harvey. *Cocktails with Cupid*, broadcast on 10 May 1941, is a fifteen-minute radio play that spawned new productions on 20 June 1942 and 30 March 1943. It should be noted, however, that although the 1942 production was listed in the *Radio Times*, correspondence in the BBC Written Archives suggests that it was cancelled and it did not appear in *The Times* radio listings.

In the case of *We Were Strangers*, the script used here is that of the stage version released to amateur companies in 1948 as a one-act play. Originally, this had been broadcast on the radio on 3 June 1938 in the forty-five minute *Three Tales of the Improbable* together with two plays not written by Durbridge. Later, as a separate twenty-minute play a new production was broadcast on 9 July 1940; and another new production as a twenty-minute play was broadcast on 16 September 1941. One final point of interest is that for the original 1938 radio version Durbridge first planned to use the title *The Enchanted Moment*.

We now turn to Durbridge's radio sketches, more than eighty of which were written between the mid-1930s and the early 1940s, with many of them lasting just a few minutes and some being little more than extended jokes. Not surprisingly most of these mini-scripts have been lost, but some have been unearthed and included in this volume.

The sketch *Mary Ann* was broadcast on 29 April 1935, included in the concert party programme *The Air-Do-Wells*, and later productions were included on 30 November 1935 in *Jack Payne's Radio Party* and on 8 January 1937 in the revue *Just Fancy That! Worth Taking* was broadcast on 30 April 1936, one of seven Durbridge sketches in *Mr. Mike Presents*, with new productions on 27 July 1936 in *Mr. Mike Presents*, on 8 January 1937 in *Just Fancy That!* and on 3 March 1937 in *The Time of March*. *Excuses* and *The Knave* were both broadcast on 2 June 1936 in *Mr. Mike Presents*, and both led to new productions. *Excuses* was included on 19 January 1937 in *Variety in Miniature*, and was later used again on 25 September 1939 in *Everything Stops for Tea*. *The Knave* also proved enduring, with a reading on 12 March 1940 in *Crime Magazine*; a new production on 7 May 1940 included in a twenty-minute programme with the story *Mark Conway Tells a Personal Tale of a Long Time Ago*; a new reading on 8 September 1941 in *Words and Music*; and a new production on 5 March 1943 in the revue *Divertissement*.

The sketch *The Ace* was broadcast on 18 August 1936 in the revue *The Tune You Heard*, and earned many new productions over the years – on 18 September 1937 in *Five O'Clock Follies*; on 16 November 1937 in the revue *Baker's Dozen*; on 11 October 1939 in *Mid-Week Matinée*; on 18 October 1940 in *Three Sketches by Francis Durbridge*, together with *Sentimental Journey* and *Hawaiian Interlude*; on 7 April 1941 in the variety programme *Divertissement*; and on 10 April 1943 in *Divertissement*.

Paul Jones was one of Durbridge's earliest sketches, going back to *Summer Showers: A Bright Interval*. This was a forty-five minute musical comedy broadcast on 17 July 1934, set in a large seaside hotel with the page calling room numbers that introduced a series of linked sketches, one of which was the first version of *Paul Jones*. Then on 12

February 1937 the separate sketch *Paul Jones* was included in *Variety in Miniature*, which resulted in several new productions – on 8 November 1939 in *Mid-Week Matinée*, on 7 August 1941 in *Lunch Interval*, on 13 June 1942 in *Cabaret*, and on 11 February 1943 in *Revue for Two*. All productions of this sketch from 1941 to 1943 were entitled *Cabaret*.

The sketch *In Training*, broadcast on 6 September 1937 in *Follow On: a Revue in Miniature*, resulted in new productions on 1 November 1939 in *Mid-Week Matinée* and on 1 September 1941 in *Everything Stops for Tea*. Both *The Customer Is Always Right* and *Parents* were on 19 October 1939 included in *Everything Stops for Tea*, with subsequently a new production of *The Customer Is Always Right* broadcast on 8 May 1942 in *Everything Stops for Tea*.

The Daily Dodge: a Family Affair is an unusual Durbridge series that could be described as an early example of a radio "soap opera", well before *Mrs Dale's Diary* and *The Archers*. A particular delight is that the eponymous daily help Mrs Dodge was played by Kathleen Harrison (1892-1995), who was born in Lancashire but made her name as cockney characters in the theatre, on the stage, on the radio, in films and on television for over half a century. *The Daily Dodge* was broadcast from 4 April to 27 June 1939 in seven episodes, although only six scripts have survived. Written by Durbridge and Archie Campbell, they were included in *For You, Madam*, "a magazine programme for every woman". This was broadcast fortnightly from 18 October 1938, but the Durbridge contribution did not begin until 4 April 1939.

All of these scripts will surely be a revelation to Durbridge enthusiasts – so enjoy them for the very first time in print!

Melvyn Barnes

Author of *Francis Durbridge: The Complete Guide* (Williams & Whiting, 2018)

This book reproduces Francis Durbridge's original script together with the list of characters and actors of the BBC programme on the dates mentioned, but the eventual broadcast might have edited Durbridge's script in respect of scenes, dialogue and character names.

Contents:

STRANGER, BEWARE!

Broadcast on BBC Radio

18th April 1941

Lyrics by Edward J. Mason
Music by Basil Hempseed
Cast includes:
Jack Melford
Marjorie Westbury
Jacques Brown
Pat Rignold
Sidney Keith
Grizelda Hervey
Charles Heslop
Joan Miller
with the Revue Orchestra and Ladies' Chorus
conducted by Hyam Greenbaum

OPEN TO:
FADE IN an orchestra playing On The Mediterranean Shore.
PAT sings and is joined by a chorus.

PAT: All aboard everyone
For the South and the sun
Train is leaving Paris right aw…ay
All the best Social Set
Needing rest (or roulette)
Are aboard this train of ours today
We're heading for the playground of France
We're shedding all out cares in advance
We're trav'lling fast on our way …
Lyon's past then Marseilles
Then at least we can say we've come to stay

On the …
Medi…terran…i…an shore
Monte Carlo or Cannes
Where each wealthy young man
Is acquainting the tan girls adore
On the Medi…terran…i..an shore
Gay abandon is rife
And the world and his wife
Are forgetting that life is a bore
There's a glamorous blonde
Who is known to be fond
Of getting div…or…ces at Reno
With a down at heel Count
Who spends any amount
Of her money when at the Casino
On the Medi…terran…i.an shore
You can have an affair and nobody will care
Mother Nature is there in the raw
On the Medi…terran…i…an shore.

3

As the music reaches a climax NICKY CARRINGTON is heard shouting from the back of the theatre.

Gradually the orchestra stops playing and the chorus, together with PAT and the conductor, break into a babble of conversation.

As NICKY draws near the conversation dies down.

PAT: (*Brightly*) What's the matter, Nicky?

NICKY: What's the matter! My dear Pat, I couldn't hear a single word at the back of the dress circle. Not a single word!

PAT: You're not supposed to, sweet. It's only the opening chorus.

NICKY: (*Irritated*) My dear, darling little sister, if the audience don't hear the opening chorus, how on earth are they to know that you're all supposed to be in Monte Carlo?

PAT: Well, this backcloth hardly looks like Brighton on a Bank Holiday!

CONDUCTOR: We're all tired, Nicky, we've been at it since ten o'clock this morning.

NICKY: Yes … Yes, all right, George. (*Raising his voice*) Break for half-an-hour everybody!

There is general laughter and conversation.

In the background a piano is heard and one of the cast commences a dance routine.

PAT leaves the stage and joins NICKY.

PAT: You look worried, Nicky.

NICKY: I don't think the show's going too well, Pat.

PAT: Well, you would take a chance with this unknown author … Robert Henshaw. No one knows anything at all about him.

NICKY: When I read the 'book', I liked it. It seemed to me to be … well … different. Now I'm wondering whether the story's got sufficient

4

	… popular appeal. Oh, it seems to be all right on the surface, I know. But I've got an awful sort of feeling that it's not quite right. I wish to goodness there was some way of finding out.
PAT:	There's the dress rehearsal, Nicky.
NICKY:	Yes, and you know only too well what dress rehearsals are! … (*Suddenly*) What is it, Mary?
MARY:	There's a gentleman to see you from The Morning Express. He said that it was rather urgent.
NICKY:	Darling, I can't see any reporters now! I told you ages ago that …
MARY:	He's not a reporter, Nicky. Here's his card.

A tiny pause.

NICKY:	(*Reading*) "Lionel Sheridan. Features Editor …" (*Thoughtfully*) Features Editor …? (*Suddenly*) Where is he? In my dressing room?
MARY:	Yes.
NICKY:	Oh, all right … I'll see him. I shan't be long, Pat.

FADE UP of the piano and the tap dance routine.

FADE COMPLETELY.

A door opens.

NICKY:	(*Pleasantly*) I'm sorry to have kept you waiting, Mr Sheridan.
SHERIDAN:	Oh, that's all right.
NICKY:	Do sit down …(*A tiny pause*) What is it … er … you wanted to see me about?
SHERIDAN:	Mr Carrington, for several weeks now, The Morning Express have published a series of

5

	articles under the general headline of 'It Happened to Me.' Each article deals with an interesting adventure or episode which, at some time or another, has befallen a person of note. Now ... er ... since you happen to be the most popular musical comedy star of the moment, we were wondering ...
NICKY:	Whether I could oblige you with a particularly exciting story? I'm sorry, Mr Sheridan, but it's not quite in my line. (*Laughing*) In any case, I wouldn't know what sort of a story would appeal to your readers.
SHERIDAN:	We'd soon tell you whether your story was likely to be a popular one or not. With a circulation of over two million it's our business to know what the people want!
NICKY:	(*Thoughtfully*) Yes. Yes, I suppose it is ... (*Suddenly*) You know ... I did have <u>one</u> rather interesting adventure about two years ago ...
SHERIDAN:	(*Interested*) Really?
NICKY:	Yes. My sister and I were appearing in cabaret in the South of France. Pat was at the Hotel Miranez and a restaurant known as The Café de Madrid. I was appearing at the Casino in Cannes. One night in the Casino ... (*Start to FADE VOICE*) ... when the place was absolutely packed to capacity and there wasn't the slightest chance of ...

FADE IN of laughter and conversation.
The conversation dies down, and there is a smattering of applause.
The applause develops, then gradually subsides.

The orchestra commences.
NICKY sings:

NICKY: Out in Caracas
          The folks in Caracas
          Will dance to Maracas
          All day
          You can't mistake 'em
          Out there when they shake 'em
          Maracas will make 'em
          All sway
          Soon as the band starts that old Rhumba beat
          The people all get on their feet

          In Caracas … they go crackers on Maracas
          Though the weather may be bakin'
          An' their arms an' legs are achin'
          When they hear Maracas shakin'
          They sing Yah – yah – yah
          De-da-de-da yah – yah – yah
          De-da-de-da yah
          In Caracas
          They go crackers on Maracas
          You just can't do nothin' with 'em
          When the band begins to give 'em
          That intoxicating rhythm
          That goes … Yah – yah – yah
          De-da-de-da yah – yah – yah
          De-da-de-da yah
          Cos out there – they don't care about sonatas
          You can keep all your sonatas
          They ain't got that beat
          There – they would show their indignation
          For they find no fascination
          In music that's sweet

In Caracas – they go crackers in Maracas
You will find they sit and slumber
Thro' a sentimental number
They just gotta have a rhumba
With its … Yah – yah – yah
De-da-de-da yah – yah – yah
De-da-de-da yah … out in Caracas

There is applause after the number.
FADE the orchestra.

PAT: They certainly seem to like you, Nicky.

NICKY: Hello, Pat! I thought you'd left for the Miranez.

PAT: Not yet, darling.

NICKY: Would you like a drink?

PAT: I don't think I've time, dear, although … (*A tiny pause*) What is it, Nicky?

NICKY: There's that girl, Pat. The one that was on the train … the one with the dark glasses … remember?

PAT: Yes. She still seems to be rather worried about something, doesn't she?

NICKY: (*Raising his voice slightly*) Pierre!

PIERRE: Monsieur?

NICKY: Have you any idea who that girl is … the one in the white dress, and wearing the dark glasses …?

PIERRE: I don't know for certain, monsieur. I have heard rumour that she is Lydia Van Tyler, but whether it is true or not, I cannot say. She is staying at the Miranez … quite alone, I believe.

NICKY: Thank you, Pierre.

PAT: (*Surprised*) Lydia Van Tyler! But … isn't she the richest girl in the world?

NICKY: Well, one of them … if not <u>the</u> richest. Got quite a reputation for loathing publicity. Why, they do

	say that when she arrived in New York for the ...

say that when she arrived in New York for the ... (*Softly*) Hello, she's going out on to the terrace.

PAT: (*Alarmed*) Nicky!

NICKY: What is it?

PAT: She took something out of her handbag. It looked to me like a revolver. Oh, but that's silly ... It couldn't possibly have been a ...

NICKY: Wait here, Pat!

FADE IN the casino orchestra.

FADE DOWN to the background.
Somewhere in the distance can be heard the faint rolling of the sea.

NICKY: (*Calmly*) I wouldn't do that if I were you!

LYDIA: (*Startled*) Oh!

NICKY: I'm sorry if I startled you. Here, let me take care of that ...

LYDIA: (*Intensely annoyed*) Please leave me alone!

NICKY: With pleasure ... once you've handed over the revolver.

LYDIA: I should esteem it a favour if you would kindly mind your own business!

NICKY: Miss Van Tyler, as a firm ... and somewhat fervent ... believer in disarmament, I must insist! The revolver ... (*A tiny pause*) ... Thank you.

LYDIA: Now, will you please leave me alone?

NICKY: (*Calmly*) Of course. Goodnight.

LYDIA: (*Surprised*) Oh, I ... didn't mean to be rude.

NICKY: Didn't you? Then that makes a difference. Cigarette?

LYDIA: (*Both amused and amazed*) I say, you're an unusual sort of person, aren't you?

A tiny pause.

NICKY: (*Quietly*) Is this thing loaded?

9

LYDIA:	Yes.
NICKY:	Then you did mean to …?
LYDIA:	Yes.
NICKY:	Judged from conventional standards that seems to make you a rather unusual sort of person too, doesn't it?
LYDIA:	(*Slightly amused*) Yes, I suppose it does. (*Seriously*) I don't know why I'm laughing, I'm sure. There's nothing very funny about it. It's really … rather tragic. By the way, you called me Miss Van Tyler just now. How did you know my name?
NICKY:	Someone told me …
LYDIA:	You're Nicky Carrington, aren't you?
NICKY:	Yes.
LYDIA:	(*After a tiny pause*) I suppose you are wondering why I attempted to commit suicide?
NICKY:	The thought had crossed my mind.
LYDIA:	It's not a very original story, I'm afraid.
NICKY:	Don't forget, this is the casino terrace at Cannes, it's not a very original setting.

LYDIA laughs.

NICKY:	Why are you laughing?
LYDIA:	You forgot to mention the sentimental music. (*A tiny pause*) I think I will have that cigarette after all.
NICKY:	Yes, of course.

NICKY lights LYDIA's cigarette.

LYDIA:	Thank you. (*Suddenly*) Mr Carrington, thanks for what you did, about the revolver, I mean. It was really rather stupid of me.
NICKY:	That's all right. We're all rather stupid at times. I once fell in love with a masseuse. (*As an*

	afterthought) Not a very good masseuse, of course.
LYDIA:	(*Laughing*) Of course. (*Suddenly she stops laughing*)
NICKY:	Are you terribly unhappy?
LYDIA:	Not unhappy ... exactly. Terribly ... desperately ... worried.
NICKY:	Why?
LYDIA:	Well ... (*She hesitates, then suddenly makes up her mind to confide in NICKY*) ... you've probably read in the newspapers that I'm engaged to marry a man named Louis Mannerheim ...
NICKY:	Louis Mannerheim?
LYDIA:	Yes. We're both very much in love and terribly happy, but unfortunately before I met Louis, I was engaged to an American named Hamilton ... Cedric Hamilton. I was young and emotional, and ... well, I'm afraid I wrote rather a lot of letters. Stupid ... sentimental ... letters ...
NICKY:	I see.
LYDIA:	Louis is a perfect dear. The kindest and sweetest man you could ever wish to meet. But he is nevertheless, and I don't deceive myself on this point, an extremely jealous sort of person. The very mention of Hamilton sends him into ...
NICKY:	(*Interrupting LYDIA*) Is Hamilton blackmailing you?
LYDIA:	Yes. (*Suddenly*) But he's not demanding money! Oh no, he's far too subtle for that. He wants me to return ... to him ...
NICKY:	M'm, sounds a pleasant sort of individual.
LYDIA:	He's staying at The Carlton in Monte Carlo. I saw him for a few moments this afternoon ... but

	it's quite hopeless … he won't listen to reason. I'm afraid he'll show Louis the …
NICKY:	Is your fiancé in Cannes?
LYDIA:	No. He's in Paris on business. I'm supposed to be joining him there on Thursday.
NICKY:	How many letters did you write to Hamilton, do you remember?
LYDIA:	Oh, yes. I remember all right. Fourteen. As a matter of fact he showed them to me this afternoon … at least he showed me the casket.
NICKY:	The casket?
LYDIA:	Yes, he always kept my letters locked in a casket … a sort of oriental deed box. You know the sort of thing. A large Chinese dragon on the lid, and a lot of strange writing all …
NICKY:	(*Thoughtfully*) Yes. I know the sort of thing … and if one of us could get hold of that deed box your troubles would be over.
LYDIA:	Oh, but that's impossible.
NICKY:	(*Suddenly*) Miss Van Tyler, do you know a restaurant on the Grande Corniche … the Café de Madrid?
LYDIA:	I've heard of it … they say it's very lovely. Why?
NICKY:	Do you think your fiancé would mind terribly if we had supper together … tomorrow night … say at about eleven?
LYDIA:	Well, I don't know. Don't forget, he's of a very jealous disposition.
NICKY:	Yes, but don't forget … he's in Paris.

They laugh.

FADE DOWN of the casino orchestra.

FADE IN of café chatter intermingled with laughter.

The Café de Madrid is a really lovely restaurant with a magnificent view of the Mediterranean.

PAT: Hello, Nicky! This is a pleasant surprise!

NICKY: (*Also surprised*) Why, hello, Pat! I thought you were at the Miranez.

PAT: No, not tonight, darling. Tomorrow and Tuesday. How did the show go down?

NICKY: Oh, pretty well. Are you nearly finished?

PAT: Two more numbers, that's all. (*Suddenly*) I say, this table is reserved for two.

NICKY: Yes ... any objections?

PAT: (*Laughing*) Not at all. Hello, what's in the parcel ... orchids?

NICKY: No, it isn't orchids! And if you don't start minding your own business, young lady, I'll see you get a pretty stiff reception!

PAT: Beast! (*Suddenly*) Oh, by the way, who do you think I bumped into this morning?

NICKY: I haven't the vaguest idea, you always seem to be bumping into somebody. Most probably Charlie McCarthy.

PAT: No, dear ... Archie Langton.

NICKY: Archie Langton! Good lord, what's he doing in Cannes?

PAT: I don't know. He's a Chief-Sergeant now ... or something like that.

NICKY: Chief-Inspector! What did he look like?

PAT: Oh, just about the same. Scotland Yard doesn't seem to have changed him a great deal. He's going to drop in the hotel one day for a drink.

NICKY: Good. (*Quietly*) I say, who's the old boy with the whiskers?

PAT: (*Amused*) Oh, that's Gustav. The orchestra leader. Quite a character.

13

NICKY: What is he … a Swiss?

PAT: I gather it rather depends on the international situation. (*Suddenly*) Well, I must fly! See you later, Nicky …

NICKY: O.K.

FADE in slight applause.
It develops, then suddenly dies down.
The orchestra starts.
PAT sings.

PAT: I've an illusion of the perfect man
           One who could mean everything to me.
           But that illusion has a fatal fascination
           Like a guiding light it seems to be.

           Will o' the Wisp where are you leading me
           Will o' the Wisp why do you seem to be
           Always so far and elusive from me.
           You lead me on blindly I follow you
           I know it's wrong. I shouldn't follow you
           Will o' the Wisp you're just fooling with me.
           It's so queer … first you're near
           Then you vanish away.
           Like the scheme … of a dream
           That is gone with the day.
           Someday I know you'll become real to me
           Will o' the Wisp when is that day to be
           Come when it may. I'll be true to you.

As the song finishes there is a burst of applause.
At this moment LYDIA arrives. She is slightly breathless.

LYDIA: I'm terribly sorry I'm late!

NICKY: Oh, that's all right.

LYDIA: (*Gazing across the balcony*) Isn't this heavenly!

14

NICKY: I've ordered dinner. What would you like to drink … to start with, I mean?

LYDIA: Gin and Italian.

NICKY: Good. Gin and Italian and … er … a champagne cocktail, waiter!

WAITER: Oui, monsieur!

LYDIA: (*Casually*) Who's that girl in the pink dress? I've seen her before somewhere, haven't I?

NICKY: It's Pat … my sister. Besides being here she's also appearing in cabaret at the Miranex.

LYDIA: Why yes, of course. That's where I've seen her. She's rather sweet, isn't she?

There is a sudden burst of applause.

The orchestra starts.

PAT, together with a chorus, sings.

PAT: Darkness and romance
            Shadows softly dance
            Night is aglow with the moon that it brings
            As its mellow rays
            Make a velvet haze
            Somewhere above as the night softly sings.
            Then there comes a moment we'll never recapture
            One moment of rapture divine.

            Music in the distance far away
            Echoing the tune our hearts are playing
            With a scented breeze the trees are swaying
            And hushed are all the words our lips are saying
            From the purple sky a silv'ry gleam
            Made the perfect end to all our dreaming
            Nature seemed to sigh … then from Heaven high above
            Love came in on a star.

15

After the song there is applause.
The orchestra continues.

LYDIA: Lovely! And what a sweet voice ... You must be very proud of her.

NICKY: Haven't you been here before?

LYDIA: No, I'm afraid I haven't. I think it's one of the loveliest restaurants I ... (*Surprised*) Hello, what's this?

NICKY: Oh, just a little present for you.

LYDIA: A little present ... for me ...?

NICKY: Yes. I always take the ... (*He is unwrapping the casket*) ... paper off ... the ...

LYDIA: (*Suddenly*) Why, it's the casket!

NICKY: I only meant to bring you the letters, but the casket was locked, my time was rather limited, and ...

LYDIA: But ... how ... did you get them?

NICKY: (*Amused*) Hamilton has a room facing a balcony. A telephone message brought him down to the restaurant, and I ... er ... climbed the balcony.

LYDIA: Climbed ... the ... balcony!

NICKY: Yes. I've had great experience with balconies. Even at Harrow I played in Romeo and Juliet.

LYDIA: (*Entranced*) I can just imagine you as Romeo.

NICKY: I'm afraid I ... er ... played Juliet.

LYDIA: (*Laughing*) Nevertheless, it was really very brave of you.

NICKY: Not in the least. At the most ... a little undignified.

LYDIA: Mr Carrington ... these letters mean so much to me ... more than you'll ever realise ... seriously how can I ever thank you?

NICKY: (*Softly*) Seriously … Miss Van Tyler … call me
           Nicky.

LYDIA laughs, a warm gentle laugh … and after a little while
NICKY too joins in the laughter.
FADE IN of the orchestra from the background.

FADE DOWN the orchestra.
CROSS FADE with a piano.
NICKY is carelessly improvising.

NICKY: I do wish Archie would hurry up. We don't want
           to stay in this beastly hotel all day!

PAT: (*Chuckling*) I say, have you seen this in the paper
           about Lucy Crossways?

NICKY: No.

PAT: She's done it!

NICKY: Done what?

PAT: Hooked him.

NICKY: Hooked whom?

PAT: That poor fish Larry Clemence. They're to be
           married next Thursday.

NICKY: You know, I always thought Lucy Crossways
           was after Archie.

PAT: Archie? He wouldn't bite.

NICKY: According to all accounts he'd one or two damn
           good nibbles!

PAT: (*Laughing*) Darling!

A tiny pause.

NICKY: Pat, do you remember that number Beatrice
           Weaver used to sing at The Ritz?

PAT: My Little Purple Diary? Why, of course.

NICKY: I thought of trying it out at the Casino. Edward's
           sent me a brand new lyric.

NICKY stops improvising and sings.

NICKY: When I was a schoolboy

Just a little kid
I kept a little diary of all the things I did
Teacher gave it to me
At an early age
And told me I must always fill up ev'ry page
Ever since that day, you know,
Tho' some of you may laugh
I still keep my diary,
Mostly bound in purple calf.

There's …
All about my present life and all about my past
The time I've been a trifle slow and just …
a trifle fast
The first time I said "Dam' it!
and the first time I said … "Blast!"
You'll find 'em in my little purple diary.
There's all the little things that chaps don't
casually confess
Like when I went mixed bathing once … and I
lost my bathing dress
The names of girl who've said "No, no!" and
those who've murmured "Ye-es."
You'll find 'em in my little purple diary.
I've taken chances
With my romances
And recorded all the chances that I took.
I took delight in
My bold handwritin'
An' I wrote the details in my little book
The time I had a drink and went completely up
the pole
And found a little girl, who'd got a most
delightful mole

Right where … no darn it all! … I couldn't tell that to a soul!
But you'll find it in my little purple diary!

There's all about my day nurse once when I was ill in bed
Who really rather lost her heart to me … or so she said
There's all about my night nurse, too … who rather lost her head!
Yeah … you'll find it in my little purple diary.
The times I've been to Paris … to Le Touquet … and Land's End
The times I've been to Reno and Miami … and Ostend
The times I've been down to Brighton for a weekend with a … friend …
You'll find 'em in my little purple diary.
If I'd been frisky
Or rather risqué
I'd write it down before I went to sleep
My friends would scold me
But teacher told me
That a true and faithful record I must keep
My teacher's words of wisdom in my memory always cling
He said … when I grew up … a lot of pleasure it would bring …
Which only goes to show that teachers don't know ev'rything …
Cos … my wife had found my little purple diary!

PAT: Excellent, Nicky! But I do wish you wouldn't try to look so frightfully witty all the time. Your eyebrows positively quiver with suppressed smartness.

NICKY: (*Laughing*) Idiot!

PAT: I say, Archie is late. It's nearly half past twelve.

NICKY: He always used to be late, even in the old days.

PAT: (*Amused*) Nicky, whatever made him join the police force?

NICKY: Don't ask me, darling. He probably fell madly in love with the Sergeant's daughter. Anyway, he doesn't seem to have done too badly for himself.

A slight pause.

PAT: (*Surprised*) I say, Nicky! Have you seen this in the paper about Lydia Van Tyler?

NICKY: No. What is it?

PAT: Listen! Listen to this … (*Reading*) "A novel feature of Countess Mannerheim's party held at The Palace Hotel, Nice, last night, was the first appearance in Europe of 'La Velzina,' the celebrated South American dancer who recently appeared before Mr and Mrs Roosevelt at a party given in their honour by the British Ambassador. It will be recalled that Countess Mannerheim was formerly Lydia Van Tyler, and that her marriage to Count Louis Mannerheim only became known to readers of The Daily News on Tuesday of this week."

NICKY: What's the date on that paper?

PAT: Saturday … January 28th … (*Surprised*) But, Nicky, she couldn't have been at that party. That was the night you went to The Café de Madrid, the night you …

NICKY: (*Softly*) Yes.

A knock is heard on the door.

PAT: Here's Archie …

NICKY: Don't keep him waiting, Pat.

The door opens.

CHIEF INSPECTOR LONGTON is not the conventional detective of fiction. He is a young man of about thirty-eight with a slightly blasé manner.

ARCHIE: Hello, Pat! I say, I'm frightfully sorry I'm late.

NICKY: That's all right, old boy. We expected it.

ARCHIE: (*Laughing*) Hello … Nicky! How are you? My word, doesn't he look fit? Still the bouncing juvenile.

NICKY: What do you mean … 'still' …?

PAT laughs.

ARCHIE: I don't know how you stage people do it. You always seem to be brimming over with health.

NICKY: Well, you don't look so bad for a flatfoot!

ARCHIE: I resent that! Chief Inspector …

NICKY: Whoops, dearie! A Chief Inspector! No, seriously, old boy, what are you doing in Cannes?

ARCHIE: Oh, I'm just here on a sort of … er … holiday.

NICKY: You can't kid us, Archie! We know our E. Phillips Oppenheim. (*At the piano. Dramatically*) Brilliant young detective meets espionage agent on Promenade des Anglais!

PAT: (*Lapsing into the same tone*) Secret documents leave for Budapest by Trans-Continental Express!

NICKY: Comrade Vastovich, Russian Envoy Extraordinary, leaves for Moscow!!!

PAT: Hitler telephones Mussolini!!!!

NICKY: (*Softly*) … and reverses the charges …

PAT: Suspicion!!!!

NICKY: Intrigue!!!!

PAT: Espionage!!!!

NICKY:	Foul play!!!!
PAT:	Send for Archie Longton!!!
NICKY:	Send for Archie Longton!!!
ARCHIE:	(*Laughing*) Still the same delightful idiots!
PAT:	(*Also laughing*) What would you like, sweet ... a sherry?
ARCHIE:	Please.
NICKY:	No, seriously, Archie, what <u>are</u> you doing in Cannes?
ARCHIE:	I'm over here on a sort of ... er ... special mission. Do you know anything about a girl who calls herself ... amongst other things ... Princess Carlento?
NICKY:	Princess Carlento? No, why do you ask?
PAT:	Is she a crook?
ARCHIE:	(*Amused*) Is she a ... Listen, Nicky, you know as well as I do that all this sort of stuff you read in books about people disguising themselves to look like someone else is just so much ballyhoo. But this girl is different. She doesn't impersonate a person ... she literally is that person ... it's absolutely uncanny!
PAT:	(*Excitedly*) Why, Nicky! This explains everything! The girl you ...
NICKY:	This Princess Carlento certainly sounds a very remarkable sort of person.
ARCHIE:	Remarkable! I'd like you to meet her, Nicky.
NICKY:	(*Slightly amused*) I'm beginning to think we ... er ... have met, Archie.
ARCHIE:	(*Puzzled*) You have met ...? Where?
NICKY:	(*Cordially*) Oh ... at the Casino ... in the moonlight ... on a terrace ...
ARCHIE:	At the Casino ... in the moonlight ... on a ter ... (*Amused*) Oh, Nicky, won't you ever grow up!

ARCHIE laughs, and after a little while NICKY laughs but it is not for the same reason.
FADE laughter.

A door opens.
COUNTESS: (*Irritated*) What is it, Francois? I'd made it perfectly clear that I didn't want to be disturbed!
The COUNTESS speaks with a slight American accent.
FRANCOIS: Pardon, madam, but there is a gentleman to see you. A Monsieur Carrington.
COUNTESS: Carrington? Ask him in here, Francois.
FRANCOIS: Yes, madam.
There is a pause.
NICKY: (*Politely*) Thank you.
FRANCOIS: Monsieur Carrington, madam.
COUNTESS: Thank you, Francois. That will be all.
The door closes.
NICKY: Countess Mannerheim?
COUNTESS: Yes.
NICKY: I don't think we've had the pleasure of meeting before, Countess.
COUNTESS: I don't think so either, and to be quite frank, I have very little time at my disposal.
NICKY: In which case you would like me to come straight to the point?
COUNTESS: By all means.
A tiny pause.
NICKY: I hope you'll forgive me if I make a personal observation?
COUNTESS: That entirely depends upon how personal it is.
NICKY: (*Suddenly*) Countess, you have been married precisely a week. Your husband is kind, generous, and terribly in love. You would in

23

fact be supremely happy if it were not for one small, but nevertheless excessively irritating, factor.

COUNTESS: What do you mean?

NICKY: (*Simply*) You are being blackmailed.

There is a pause.

COUNTESS: How did you know?

NICKY: It's true, isn't it?

COUNTESS: (*Softly*) Yes. It is, it's quite true. Before my marriage I was, of course, Lydia Van Tyler and ... (*Suspiciously*) Oh, I'm beginning to see daylight! So you're the person behind this blackmailing stunt!

NICKY: Countess, believe it or not, I'm here to help you. Indeed, I'm here to give you my personal assurance that there is absolutely nothing for you to worry about.

COUNTESS: Say, is this on the level?

NICKY: (*Amused*) Absolutely. Now supposing you tell me precisely what happened?

COUNTESS: Well, I'm afraid it's rather a crazy sort of story. You see, before I married Count Mannerheim, I was engaged to an American called Cedric Hamilton. Cedric was a perfect dear, but ever so, so frightfully sentimental! Naturally, however, I was very much in love with him at the time. Well, anyway, to cut a long story short, I wrote Cedric some letters – pretty childish and somewhat sentimental letters – I guess. When we broke off our engagement I asked him for the letters back because I knew that if Louis ever saw them – that is my present husband – there'd be an awful lot of explaining to do. Cedric refused to return them, however,

24

and suddenly became stupidly sentimental about the whole business. He even carried the letters about with him in a funny sort of Chinese casket. Well, last week the letters were stolen … stolen by a girl who calls herself Princess Carlento.

NICKY: Then you've heard from Princess Carlento?

COUNTESS: Three days ago. She wants thirty-five thousand pounds.

NICKY: Phew!

COUNTESS: … If I don't deliver the money by eight o'clock tonight she threatens to send Louis the letters. And she will, too. I know a determined sort of person when I meet one!

NICKY: Well, that's where you're mistaken, Countess! What arrangements did you make with Princess Carlento?

COUNTESS: I promised to meet her at The Miranez Hotel in Cannes. She told me to ask for Room 706.

NICKY: (*Thoughtfully*) Room … 706 …

COUNTESS: Mr Carrington, what did you mean when you said that … there was absolutely nothing for me to worry about?

NICKY: I meant, my dear Countess, that there is absolutely nothing for you to worry about.

COUNTESS: But the letters? What about the letters?

NICKY: The letters are in safe keeping, Countess, I assure you.

COUNTESS: (*Quietly amazed*) You mean … that … you have the letters?

NICKY: I mean that if you meet me at The Mirenz Hotel this evening for supper, say at eleven o'clock, I shall be very happy to hand them over to you.

COUNTESS: Without … er … any strings?

25

NICKY: Without any strings, Countess ... I promise. Although I hope you won't hold me responsible for a certain proposition which might ... er ... enter my head at the sight of you in a gown.

Slow FADE IN of an orchestra.

FADE to background with typical restaurant noises.
The orchestra stops.
There is a smattering of applause.
A pause.

PAT: Hello, Nicky.

NICKY: Hello, darling ... you went down very well tonight.

PAT: Yes. They seem to like me here better than at The Café de Madrid.

NICKY: What time do you make it, Pat?

PAT: It's about ten-thirty. Do you think she'll turn up all right ...?

NICKY: Who? The Countess ...? She'll turn up, don't you worry.

PAT: (*Slightly anxious*) Have you got the letters, Nicky?

NICKY: (*Casually*) Why, yes ... of course.

PAT: (*Puzzled*) I don't understand this, Nicky! First you meet this Princess Carlento who is impersonating Countess Mannerheim ... or Lydia Van Tyler that was ... and she persuades you to steal a casket which contains letters which belong to the real Countess Mannerheim ...

NICKY: ... or Lydia Van Tyler that was ...

PAT: Then ... to crown everything ... instead of handing over the letters you simply hand over the empty casket.

NICKY: That's right.

PAT: Then you must have guessed that the first girl wasn't the real Lydia Van Tyler?

NICKY: (*Amused*) Wait in the lounge, Pat! I'll join you later.

FADE IN the noise of an elevator.

FADE the background restaurant chatter and noises completely.

The elevator stops.

The door slides open.

LIFT BOY: Room 706 … Second door on the left, monsieur.

NICKY: Thank you.

FADE IN the noise of the elevator.

FADE DOWN.

A pause.

NICKY: Good evening, Miss Van Tyler, or should I say, Princess Carlento?

LYDIA: (*Astonished*) What are you doing here?

NICKY: Remember me? Nicky Carrington … the S.O.S, guy. Damsels in distress a speciality. (*Suddenly*) Ah, I see you still have the casket!

LYDIA: What is it you want?

NICKY: Oh, just a friendly chat. I get desperately lonely at times, but surely I explained all that to you at the Café de Madrid.

LYDIA: (*Amused*) I haven't a great deal of time on my hands, and I'm expecting someone, so …

NICKY: Ah, yes! Countess Mannerheim. Now there's an interesting girl for you! You know, Princess, I don't think your impersonation was quite … er … tonish enough.

LYDIA: Don't you? It seemed to do the trick all right.

NICKY: Trick? What … trick?

LYDIA: Well, after all, you did get me the letters, didn't you?

NICKY:	I got you a casket. A very nice one too. It cost me six hundred francs.
LYDIA:	(*Staggered*) Six hundred … francs!
NICKY:	(*Politely*) Yes, do you think it was too dear?
LYDIA:	(*Completely amazed*) You mean to say that … this … isn't the casket with the letters?
NICKY:	Why no, of course not! Haven't you opened it yet?
LYDIA:	(*Weakly*) No … it's … locked.
NICKY:	Oh, yes! I insisted on a lock. I remember showing the original casket to the man in the shop and …
LYDIA:	The … original …? Then you did get the letters?
NICKY:	But of course. I'm delivering them to Miss Van Tyler tonight.
LYDIA:	For … what?
NICKY:	Not for thirty-five thousand pounds, Princess, I assure you. I may be a little old fashioned, but somehow there's a nasty sort of taste about blackmail … or don't you agree?

A knock is heard.

The door opens.

CONCIERGE: Princess Carlento?

LYDIA: Yes … (*Suddenly*) Oh, what lovely flowers!

CONCIERGE: Shall I put them in the vase, madame, or …?

LYDIA: No, it's all right, I'll take them! (*Excitedly*) Aren't they adorable!

CONCIERGE: I was asked to deliver this card, madame.

LYDIA: Thank you!

NICKY: Here we are …

CONCIERGE: Merci, monsieur.

The door closes.

LYDIA:	Aren't they absolutely lovely! (*Reading the card*) "From Nicky Carrington."
NICKY:	I hope you're fond of orchids?
LYDIA:	That's really very sweet … very sweet of you.
NICKY:	And you forgive me for not falling for your … er … little plot?
LYDIA:	But of course! (*Suddenly*) Here … take … the casket! It might be useful for keeping cigarettes in …
NICKY:	(*Amused*) If I can get the lock undone!
LYDIA:	Well, after all, you did pay six hundred francs for it!

They laugh.

FADE IN orchestra and restaurant noises.
The orchestra reprises Will o' the Wisp.

PAT:	Hello, Nicky, where on earth have you been?
NICKY:	Has the Countess arrived?
PAT:	Not yet. But it's nearly time you were leaving for the … (*Suddenly*) Why … Why, good gracious, that's the casket!
NICKY:	(*Amused*) That's right, Pat.
PAT:	But … But where did you get it from? Nicky … not from … Princess Carlento?
NICKY:	Yes.
PAT:	(*Suspiciously*) Nicky Carrington … you didn't fall for her trick that night by any chance?
NICKY:	(*Amused*) I'm afraid so, Pat.
PAT:	(*Staggered*) But … But the letters? You don't mean to say they're in … that … casket?
NICKY:	I'm afraid so. (*He chuckles*)
PAT:	Then … then she's just handed them … back to you?

29

NICKY: (*Greatly amused*) I'm afraid so, my dear! I'm afraid so! (*Suddenly calling*) Oh, concierge!

CONCIERGE: Monsieur?

NICKY: About those orchids. You might … er … charge them to … Room 706.

CONCIERGE: Room 706? Why, certainly, monsieur!

FADE UP of orchestra.

FADE DOWN very slowly.

FADE IN of LIONEL SHERIDAN laughing.

NICKY: (*Anxiously*) So, what do you think?

SHERIDAN: (*Enthusiastically*) What do I think? Why, Mr Carrington, it's terrific! I've never heard a story with so much charm and originality.

NICKY: You … you really think so?

SHERIDAN: Why … why, it's colossal!

NICKY: (*With a sigh of relief*) Well, I'm glad to hear you say so, Mr Sheridan. But I'm afraid you won't be able to publish it.

SHERIDAN: Oh?

NICKY: No. You see, the story I've just told you doesn't happen to be true. It's the story of Stranger, Beware – the new show I'm rehearsing.

SHERIDAN: Then … why did you tell it to me?

NICKY: Because I wanted your reaction. I wanted to know whether in your opinion – in an expert's opinion – the story was a really … popular one.

SHERIDAN: Popular! Why, of course! It's got everything, Mr Carrington! Gaiety! Sparkle! Wit! Sunshine! Romance! Good lord, what more can anyone want?

NICKY: Then you think it'll be a success?

SHERIDAN:	A success? You'll pack 'em in! With a story like that you can't possibly go wrong!
NICKY:	(*Brightly*) I hope you're right, Mr Sheridan. I hope you're right!

The door opens.

CONDUCTOR:	All ready for the finale, Nicky?
NICKY:	O.K. ... I'm coming, George. (*To SHERIDAN*) Perhaps you'd like to stay and see a little of the rehearsal?
SHERIDAN:	Yes, I would ... rather. (*Suddenly*) Oh, there's just one point, Mr Carrington ...
NICKY:	Yes?
SHERIDAN:	About that story you told me ... Of course I ... er ... may be prejudiced.
NICKY:	Prejudiced? Why ...?
SHERIDAN:	Well, you see ... my nom-de-plume happens to be Henshaw. I ... er ... wrote it.
NICKY:	(*Staggered*) You ... you wrote it!

NICKY starts chuckling and as the situation gradually dawns on him the chuckling develops into uproarious laughter.

FADE the laughter to the stage for a musical finale with the orchestra and chorus.

THE END

THE HOUSE ON

THE CORNER

Broadcast on BBC Radio

24th December 1941

CAST:

Taxi driver . . . . William Hughes
Nigel . . . . Godfrey Baseley
Cabby . . . . .Lester Mudditt
Linda . . . . .Mary Jones
Man at party . .Philip Garston-Jones
Girl at party . . . .Marjorie Westbury
Other parts played by
members of the cast
with Jack Wilson at the piano
and the BBC Midland Light Orchestra
conducted by Richard Crean

OPEN TO:

An orchestra is playing the theme waltz.
From this the music of the period develops: 1904 – then to the present day.
Through this selection the introductory announcements are made ...
When the orchestra have returned to the waltz, there is a SLOW FADE for the voice of THE MAN.

MAN: At precisely four-fifteen on Christmas Eve in the year Nineteen-Forty a young man by the name of Nigel Harwood took a taxi from Waterloo Station to an address in Mount Street.

FADE UP of music then CROSS FADE to the taxi.
The taxi stops and the door opens and closes.

DRIVER: (*Puzzled*) Is this right, sir?

NIGEL: Yes, this is quite right. How much do you want?

DRIVER: Well, there's two-an'-nine on the meter, sir.

NIGEL: I see. Well ... here we are.

DRIVER: (*Pleased*) Oh, thank you, sir. An' the compliments of the season.

NIGEL: Thank you.

DRIVER: I suppose that was the house you meant, sir, on the other side of the road?

NIGEL: Yes, that was the house I meant. Goodnight.

DRIVER: Goodnight, sir.

The taxi departs.
As the taxi fades we hear, in the background, a street choir singing Christmas songs.
The choir gradually draws closer.
They finish a song and NIGEL is thanked for a contribution.

SINGER: Thank you, sir. Thank you very much, sir.

NIGEL:	Forgive me asking, but do you by any chance happen to know a song called Christmas in the Rain.
SINGER:	…. Christmas in the Rain? No. No, I'm afraid I don't sir.
2nd SINGER:	(*Laughing*) Christmas in the Rain? Shades of Cecile Mannering. (*She sings the first few bars of the song*)
NIGEL:	Yes … Yes, that's it!

The girl continues to sing the song, and she is joined by the rest of her friends. The song finishes and the girl laughs …

| 2nd SINGER: | (*Amused*) I don't think we quite remembered the tune …! |
| NIGEL: | You not only remembered it perfectly, but you sang it perfectly as well … thank you. |

The choir start to sing the song again and pass down the street out of hearing.

There is a slight pause.

A POLICEMAN slowly approaches.

POLICEMAN:	Good evening, sir.
NIGEL:	Good evening, officer.
POLICEMAN:	(*Puzzled*) Is … Is anything the matter, sir?
NIGEL:	Anything the matter? No … No, not that I'm aware of.
POLICEMAN:	(*Suspiciously*) I've … er … I've been watching you, sir.
NIGEL:	Indeed?
POLICEMAN:	Yes … Yes, er … what's the idea …? What are you staring at?
NIGEL:	At this house, officer … or rather … what there is left of it.
POLICEMAN:	Well, I … er … I think I should move on if I were you, sir.

NIGEL: Would you? Oh, well … perhaps you're right.

POLICEMAN: (*Politely*) No offence, sir, but we've had rather strict instructions about these blitzed houses.

NIGEL: Yes. Yes, of course.

POLICEMAN: I don't know whether you remember this house or not, sir? It used to be rather pleasant. It had grey shutters and … (*Thoughtfully*) … or were they green? (*Surprised*) Now … that's funny! I must have passed here hundreds of times, and I can't even remember what colour the shutters were!

NIGEL: They were brown.

POLICEMAN: Brown?

NIGEL: Yes.

POLICEMAN: Then you knew this house, sir … before it was bombed, I mean?

There is a pause.

NIGEL: My father was always very fond of it.

FADE IN of the orchestra playing the theme waltz.

SLOW FADE to the background for the voice of THE MAN.

MAN: At precisely four-fifteen on Christmas Eve in the year Nineteen-o'-four, a young man by the name of Nigel Harwood took a hansom cab from Waterloo Station to an address in Mount Street.

FADE UP of music then CROSS FADE to the hansom cab.
The cab continues for a little while, then finally comes to a standstill.

DRIVER: (*Pleasantly*) Here we are, sir! Steady, boy! Steady!!

NIGEL: What's the fare, cabby?

DRIVER: Oh, er … half-a-crown, sir.

NIGEL: Here we are … you can keep the change.

DRIVER: Oh, thank you kindly, sir … an' a merry Christmas.

NIGEL: Thank you.

The hansom cab departs.

There is a background of street noises.

Somewhere in the distance a choir is singing carols.

The sound of an approaching carriage can be heard.

It draws to a standstill.

NIGEL: (*Excited*) Linda! Then … Then you did get my message? (*With a sigh of relief*) Oh, darling!

LINDA: (*Laughing*) What's all the mystery about, Nigel? And … And, darling, why the change of plan? Surely it would have been much better if we'd met at Gunter's …

NIGEL: (*Thrilled*) No! No, my sweet! Hello, Barker! A merry Christmas!

BARKER: Thank you, sir. And a very merry Christmas to you too, Mr Nigel … Is that all, Miss Linda …?

LINDA: Yes, that's all, Barker … thank you.

BARKER: Good day, sir. Good day, Miss Linda … (*Suddenly*) Oh! Oh, I was forgetting … I … I thought perhaps the … er … door key might be of … er … some service, miss, just in case you …

LINDA: (*Laughing – amazed*) Barker! Barker, how on earth did you manage to get the key?

BARKER: Oh, it's rather a long story, Miss Linda … (*Chuckling*) Some other time, perhaps, eh, sir? Goodbye, sir! Goodbye, Miss Linda!

BARKER calls the horses and the carriage departs.

There is a slight pause.

LINDA: Well, Nigel …

NIGEL: A merry Christmas, Linda!

LINDA: A merry Christmas, Nigel! And now …

NIGEL: And now, perhaps, I'll tell you why I wanted you to meet in Mount Street instead of … at the tea shop. Come … let's cross the road, Linda!

LINDA: (*Faintly alarmed*) Darling – Darling, we're not going for a walk?

NIGEL: No, we're not going for a walk …

LINDA: You've … You've got the theatre tickets … all right?

NIGEL: (*Amused*) Yes, I've got the theatre tickets … all right. (*Suddenly*) Ah! Ah, here we are … Now, tell me … Linda Marshall … what do you think of that house? No! No … the one on the corner … the empty house …

LINDA: (*Puzzled*) But – But I think it's charming. I've always thought so … you know that.

NIGEL: Yes, I know that.

LINDA: (*Gently*) Nigel … Nigel, what is it?

NIGEL: Next year, my sweet, God willing … there will be lights in that house, and music, and laughter … your laughter, Linda Marshall.

LINDA: What – What do you mean?

NIGEL: The house on the corner is ours, Linda. I – I bought it this morning.

FADE IN of the orchestra playing the theme waltz.

FADE DOWN the orchestra.

MAN: And so, on Christmas Eve, in the year Nineteen-o'-four, Nigel Harwood and Linda Marshall went to the theatre. And in a box at the Apollo they heard, for the first time …

39

FADE IN of orchestra and chorus together with Cecile Mannering singing the song previously spoken about.

When the song is nearly finished we FADE from the stage to the private box.

As the song finishes on FADE there is applause.

It is the theatre interval.

NIGEL: Happy, Linda?

LINDA: Yes, I'm very happy, Nigel.

NIGEL: What were you thinking about, just now …?

LINDA: Just now? (*With a little laugh*) I – I didn't realise that you were watching me. I was thinking of how twelve months can make such a difference.

NIGEL: Such a difference?

LINDA: To the life of a person, I mean. Twelve months ago we hardly knew one another, Nigel, do you realise that?

NIGEL: (*Thoughtfully*) Yes. We hardly knew one another and yet … I asked you to dance.

LINDA: (*As always, amused at the recollection*) I'd never met anyone quite so self-possessed!

FADE IN slowly of the orchestra playing a gay waltz …

NIGEL: Self-possessed? Oh, if only you'd known how my knees were shaking with terror, and my heart positively pounding at the thought that … you might turn me down.

LINDA: (*Laughing*) You knew perfectly well that I should dance with you, the moment you came across the dance floor.

NIGEL: Yes. Yes, I think perhaps … I did.

FADE IN of the orchestra playing the gay waltz.

A ball is in progress.

Dancers are swirling and pirouetting to the music.

The music FADES DOWN for the following speech:

NIGEL: Miss Marshall, I believe.

LINDA: (*With a start of surprise*) Yes.

NIGEL: May I have the pleasure of this waltz, Miss
            Marshall?

LINDA: (*Hesitatingly*) Well …

NIGEL: My name is Nigel Harwood. We met about six
            months ago at my uncle's house … (*Almost as
            an afterthought*) … in Richmond.

LINDA: Ah … Ah, yes! (*With an amused twinkle*) You
            dance well, Mr Harwood?

NIGEL: Divinely.

LINDA: Then you shall have the pleasure.

FADE UP of the orchestra playing the gay waltz.

When the waltz is nearly over the orchestra FADES.

FADE IN of LINDA laughing.

LINDA: And the very next day you took me to Gunter's
            tea shop, do you remember?

NIGEL: I shall never forget. You had teacakes, a scone,
            and three chocolate eclairs. I remember saying to
            myself, almost as if it were yesterday: "This is
            dreadful, I'm falling madly in love with a woman
            with an enormous appetite."

LINDA: Twelve months ago! It hardly seems twelve days
            ago, Nigel.

NIGEL: No: when one is in love, time passes very
            quickly, Linda.

LINDA: Then I hope that, whatever the future may have
            in store for us, about the past at any rate, we shall
            always be able to say … it seems only yesterday
            …

NIGEL: That's a very sweet thought, Linda … if a shade
            sentimental.

*The orchestra starts the opening to the second half of the
show.*

There is a smattering of applause.

The orchestra continues.

There is a pause before LINDA speaks.

LINDA: (*Quietly*) Nigel ...

NIGEL: Yes?

LINDA: (*Changing her mind*) Oh ... it's all right, darling.

NIGEL: What were you going to say? (*After a pause*) Linda, please ...

LINDA: I was going to say ... I wonder where we shall be ... at this time ... twelve months from today?

NIGEL: Christmas Eve, Nineteen-o—five ... at a quarter to ten ... I wonder?

FADE IN of the theatre orchestra.

FADE DOWN of the orchestra.

It is a very SLOW FADE and from the background we hear:

NIGEL: Next year, my sweet, God willing ... there will be lights in that house, and music, and laughter ... your laughter, Linda Marshall.

Continue the SLOW FADE of the orchestra and CROSS FADE with LINDA laughing.

FADE IN of the next scene.

LINDA and NIGEL are dining together alone.

LINDA: (*Laughing: highly amused*) Sit down! Sit down, Nigel!!!!

NIGEL: I won't sit down! I insist ... I positively insist on making a speech!

LINDA: What's the good of making a speech, darling, when there's no one to listen to you?

NIGEL: (*Overacting*) Ah!!! Ah!!! But that's when I'm at my best, Linda, when words positively exude from me! Indeed, there are times, my dear – in the privacy of the bath for example – when your husband is nothing more or less than an inspired fountain of eloquence.

LINDA: (*Unmoved*) That's a very bad impersonation of Martin Harvey. Sit down, Nigel.

NIGEL: Yes, my dear.

NIGEL sits.

LINDA: (*Giggling*) You are a fool …

NIGEL: (*After a pause: seriously*) Are you ever sorry, Linda?

LINDA: Sorry?

NIGEL: About us …

LINDA: What do you mean, Nigel?

NIGEL: Are you ever sorry that you married a fool who … can't even do a very good impersonation of Martin Harvey?

There is a tiny pause.

LINDA: You're not such a fool, Nigel!

NIGEL: (*Chuckling*) Oh … Oh, so you've found that out already, have you?

LINDA: Last year, my dear, when we stood on the corner of Mount Street, looking across to the house, you said: "Next year, my sweet, God willing … there will be lights in that house, and music … and laughter …"

NIGEL: And I was right …

LINDA: Yes, as always, you were right, Nigel. (*After a tiny pause*) Why are you smiling?

NIGEL: I was thinking of what Brian Howard said, the first day he came here.

LINDA: (*Faintly amused*) For a child of six I do find Brian so very precocious.

NIGEL: Nevertheless, he has an uncanny knack of hitting the nail on the head. We were standing by the window – Margaret, Brian and I – and Margaret

43

asked: "What made you buy this house, Nigel?" And Brian said: "I'm sure Uncle Nigel bought it because it was on the corner."

LINDA: Did you buy it because it was on the corner, Nigel?

NIGEL: I bought it because it was on the corner, because it had brown shutters ... and because the first time I kissed you was in Mount Street.

LINDA: (*Deeply moved*) Now – Now you're making me cry. And – And I didn't want to cry, not on Christmas Eve ...

NIGEL: (*Laughing*) Didn't you, my sweet? Well, here's something that might help to dry your tears.

NIGEL produces his surprise Christmas present.

LINDA: (*Astonished*) Why ... Why, Nigel!

A tiny pause.

NIGEL: You like it?

LINDA: It's the loveliest necklace I've ever seen ...

NIGEL: (*Suddenly*) Here ... Here ... Let me put it on for you ...

NIGEL rises from the table.

A pause.

NIGEL: There ... There we are ...

LINDA: (*Thrilled*) Oh ... Oh, Nigel!

NIGEL: And now, whether you approve or not, Linda, I'm going to make a speech.

LINDA: (*Gently – amused*) Oh, darling! Not another!

NIGEL: (*With his mock Shakespearean manner*) The first time we came to this house, and no doubt you recollect the occasion just as well as I ... (*He stops speaking*)

Outside, in the hall, the clock is chiming. It is a quarter to ten. After a pause.

LINDA:	(*Quietly*) It's a quarter to ten. Do you remember …?
NIGEL:	Yes.
LINDA:	Last year we were in a box at the Apollo Theatre and …
NIGEL:	Yes, I remember.
LINDA:	It hardly seems twelve months ago, Nigel.
NIGEL:	No; when one is in love, time passes very quickly, Linda.
LINDA:	(*Faintly surprised*) You said that before.
NIGEL:	Yes. Yes, I believe I did.

A tiny pause.

LINDA:	(*Thoughtfully*) Christmas Eve, Ninteen-o'-five at a quarter to ten …
NIGEL:	(*Quietly – with sincerity*) And this time you don't have to tell me what you are thinking, Linda, because I know. When I bought this house, and that too, only seems like yesterday, I had in my mind – and in my heart too, I believe – all the hours and the weeks and God willing, the years that we should spend together here. This is a strange house, Linda, in many ways; and one could not really argue with the friend who, for the want of a better term, called it ugly.
LINDA:	(*Interrupting NIGEL – softly*) Oh, no!
NIGEL:	For indeed it is ugly, Linda. The shutters want painting, there is a strange – and one must confess – a rather exotic wallpaper in the bathroom, and the hall is so dark that by tea-time, even in the summer, the gas is nearly always burning. But these things can be changed, as indeed, no doubt they will be. But what cannot be changed, Linda, is the warmth and the friendliness which we both felt the first day we

came here. This house, with all its faults, Linda, is a house very dear to our hearts. Last year, in a box at the Apollo you said: "I wonder where we shall be … at this time … twelve months from today." That was Christmas Eve, Nineteen-o'-four and now this is Christmas Eve, Nineteen-o'-five. Tonight you nearly said very much the same thing about our future, but I'm glad that you didn't. For to me, dearest heart, the present is so perfect and the future – with all its hidden laughter, disappointments, tears and music – will come soon enough.

LINDA: (*Deeply moved*) Dear Nigel, you made your speech after all.

FADE IN of the orchestra playing the theme music.

After the theme music the orchestra plays a selection which covers the period from Nineteen-o'-seven to Nineteen-twenty-three. During this selection the chorus is heard.

FADE on the closing number of the selection.

MAN: It is Christmas Eve, Nineteen-twenty-three, and in the drawing room of their house in Mount Street, Nigel and Linda Harwood are giving a party …

GIRL: My dear, I could have died! And in Venice of all places!

1st MAN: I beg your pardon?

GIRL: I said: "And in Venice of all places."

1st MAN: I'm afraid I can't hear you very well, there's such a noise.

GIRL: (*Shouting*) I said: "And in Venice of all places."

1st MAN: (*Who hasn't heard a word*) Oh, quite.

FADE to another part of the room.

2nd GIRL: (*Very, very coy*) Could I have another cocktail?

2nd MAN:	But of course.
2nd GIRL:	Just a teeny-weeny one.
2nd MAN:	A Bronx?
2nd GIRL:	Would that be too, too wicked of me?
2nd MAN:	No. No, of course not. (*Under his breath*) My God, and she's had six!

FADE to another part of the room.

NIGEL:	(*Quietly*) I'm sorry, Linda.
LINDA:	Sorry?
NIGEL:	(*Irritated*) About this frightful party, I never dreamt it would develop like this.
LINDA:	(*Faintly amused*) Didn't you?
NIGEL:	I … I simply invited Brian round for a cocktail … and this happened!
LINDA:	(*Playfully*) This always does happen when you invite Brian, I should have warned you, Nigel!

There is a sudden stir amongst the guests.

LINDA:	Talk of the devil, here he is!
NIGEL:	And not before time either!

There is a great deal of chatter and laughter.

BRIAN:	(*Rather breathlessly*) Nigel! Linda, my sweet, am I terribly late?
NIGEL:	You did say eight o'clock, Brian!
BRIAN:	I tried to get away from the theatre, I did my best to get away from the theatre. All the time that I was rehearsing I kept saying to myself, over and over again: "Nigel and Linda are furious!" … "Nigel and Linda are furious!" … "Nigel and Linda are furious!" … apart from anything else it became excessively monotonous. (*Aside*) Thank you, darling, I'd like a sidecar.
NIGEL:	(*Quietly*) Brian, I don't know whether you realise it or not but …

NIGEL is interrupted by the 2ND GIRL.

47

2nd GIRL: Brian, my sweet!

BRIAN: Why, Tony! How long have you been here? Darling, this is heaven! Where's Simon?

2nd GIRL: He's in Grindelwald.

BRIAN: Is that wise?

2nd MAN: Hello, Brian!

BRIAN: Hello, Monty!!

2nd MAN: Brian, would you mind terribly if we asked you to sing Parisian Pierrot?

BRIAN: I should mind terribly if you didn't!

NIGEL: (*Softly; but firmly*) Brian, listen!!!

A tiny pause.

BRIAN: Why – why, what is it, Nigel?

NIGEL: (*Annoyed*) In a moment of weakness, and because once, many years ago, I had a great affection for your mother, I invited you here tonight … on Christmas Eve … for a cocktail.

LINDA: Nigel, please! (*To BRIAN*) Darling, could you get rid of all these people?

BRIAN: (*Staggered*) Why? Why, Linda, I'm so frightfully sorry! (*Suddenly*) I shall sing very loud, and slightly out of tune, which will give you both an admirable opportunity to slip away. If you return in precisely fifteen minutes, I give you my word that, apart from my weary figure at the piano, you will find the house utterly deserted and the silver quite intact.

LINDA: (*Gently*) Thank you, darling!

BRIAN crosses to the piano.

He plays and sings, to the delight of those present, Parisian Pierrot.

When he is about to repeat the number, FADE COMPLETELY.

FADE IN of BRIAN playing a sentimental waltz.
The guests have departed and he is quite alone.
LINDA and NIGEL return.

LINDA: So they've all gone! Did you have any trouble
           with them, Brian?

BRIAN: I never have trouble, at least – not with people.
           That's one of the advantages of being notorious.

LINDA and NIGEL laugh.

NIGEL: Here's a cocktail, Brian.

BRIAN stops playing.

BRIAN: Oh, thank you.

NIGEL: Linda …

LINDA: Thank you, darling.

In the hall outside the clock is chiming. It is a quarter to ten.

NIGEL: It's – It's a quarter to ten, Linda.

LINDA: Yes. Merry Christmas, Linda!

BRIAN: God bless!

NIGEL: God bless!

LINDA: God bless!

Their glasses touch.
BRIAN continues to play the sentimental waltz.

The sentimental waltz is taken over by the orchestra.
*From this waltz the orchestra plays a selection which covers
the period from Nineteen-twenty-three to Nineteen-thirty-nine.*
FADE on the closing number of the selection.

MAN: It is a quarter to ten on Christmas Eve, Nineteen-
           thirty-nine. Linda is in the drawing room of the
           house in Mount Street.

FADE orchestra completely and FADE IN of a piano.
LINDA is playing rather slowly a composition by Chopin.
While she is playing the clock in the hall chimes.
The front door opens and closes.
NIGEL enters the drawing room.

The piano stops.

NIGEL:	(*Taking off his coat*) I haven't been very long.
LINDA:	No. Is it cold outside?
NIGEL:	M'm – fairly. The searchlights are out.
LINDA:	Yes, I expect they are. I've poured you out a glass of port, Nigel.
NIGEL:	Ah, thank you, my dear.
LINDA:	Did you walk far?
NIGEL:	No … No, just round the block. Brian hasn't telephoned?
LINDA:	No, darling. I daresay it's rather difficult to get through.
NIGEL:	Yes. Yes, I expect it is. (*After a pause*) Well, here we are, Linda … Christmas Eve, Nineteen-thirty-nine, at a quarter to ten.
LINDA:	And this time <u>you</u> don't have to tell me what you are thinking, Nigel, because I know.
NIGEL:	I was thinking of the night we went to the Apollo … d'you remember? We sat in a box together and held hands.
LINDA:	(*Softly*) We can still hold hands, Nigel.
NIGEL:	Yes … thank God …
LINDA:	Here's your port.
NIGEL:	A merry Christmas, Linda. God bless!
LINDA:	A merry Christmas, Nigel. God bless!

Their glasses touch.

There is a FADE IN of the orchestra playing the theme waltz.

When the waltz is nearly finished it FADES DOWN for:

POLICEMAN:	I don't know whether you remember this house or not, sir? It used to be rather pleasant. It had grey shutters and …

	(*Thoughtfully*) … or were they green? (*Surprised*) Now … that's funny! I must have passed here hundreds of times and I can't even remember what colour the shutters were!
NIGEL:	They were brown.
POLICEMAN:	Brown?
NIGEL:	Yes.
POLICEMAN:	Then you knew this house, sir … before it was bombed … I mean?

There is a pause.

| NIGEL: | My father was always very fond of it. |

FADE UP of the orchestra playing the theme waltz.

FADE DOWN for:

| NIGEL: | Next year, my sweet, God willing … there will be lights in that house, and music and laughter … your laughter, Linda Marshall. |

FADE UP of the orchestra.

FADE DOWN for:

| LINDA: | And the very next day you took me to Gunter's tea shop, do you remember? |
| NIGEL: | I shall never forget. You had two teacakes, a scone, and three chocolate eclairs. I remember saying to myself, almost as if it were yesterday: "This is dreadful, I'm falling madly in love with a woman with an enormous appetite." |

FADE UP of the orchestra.

FADE DOWN for:

| LINDA: | Then I hope that, whatever the future may have in store for us, about the past at any |

rate, we shall always be able to say … "It seems only yesterday." …

FADE IN of the orchestra …

THE END

COCKTAILS WITH CUPID

Broadcast on BBC Radio

10th May 1941

CAST:

Terry Slade . . . . . Marjorie Westbury
Sydney Cupid . . . . . . Alan Robinson
Arthur Shackleton . . . .Michael Lynd
with
Jack Wilson and his Versatile Five

A new production was scheduled for 20 June 1942, according to the *Radio Times*. The above characters were credited respectively to Marjorie Westbury, Jack Morrison and Gerald Martin (a pseudonym of producer Martyn C. Webster), but correspondence in the BBC Written Archives suggests that it was cancelled and it did not appear in *The Times* radio listings.

Another new production was broadcast on 30 March 1943, featuring Marjorie Westbury, Sydney Tafler and Lewis Stringer respectively.

OPEN TO:

An orchestra is playing These Foolish Things.

ANNOUNCER: Cocktails with Cupid ... an interlude of words and music. The scene is the cocktail bar of a large cosmopolitan hotel.

The orchestra finish the number. There is a smattering of applause.
TERRY SLADE arrives at the cocktail bar. She is about twenty-seven.
TERRY: Hello ... and how's Cupid this evening?
SYDNEY CUPID is the cocktail attendant. A philosophical cockney.
CUPID: Why, hello, Miss Slade! This is a pleasant surprise!
TERRY: Is it?
CUPID: Nothing wrong I hope, miss?
TERRY: No, nothing wrong, Cupid. Mix me a dry Martini.
CUPID: Certainly, miss.
TERRY: Well, do you think you'll like it here ...?
CUPID: Yes, I think so, miss. It takes a bit o' getting used to o' course. Not quite the same as the Minerva Hotel, you know, miss.
TERRY: No, I suppose it isn't.
A tiny pause.
CUPID: Miss Slade, I 'ope you'll forgive me if I take the liberty of speaking my mind.
TERRY: It entirely depends what's on your mind, Cupid.

CUPID: Well, miss ... it's about this 'Cupid' business. I was wondering if you could see your way towards ... er ... well ... in a manner o' speaking, starting a new fashion?

TERRY: (*Puzzled*) Perhaps I'm a little dense, but ...

CUPID: I'll elucidate, miss ... if I have your permission?

TERRY: You have my permission, Cupid.

CUPID: In every job I've been in, miss, I've always been called Cupid. Now, since I've only been 'ere a couple of weeks, I'd rather like to start off on a different footing.

TERRY: But isn't Cupid your name?

CUPID: Oh, yes, it's my name ... Sydney Cupid. But the point is this, miss. I'm not a chicken any longer, and well ... for a grown man with three kids and a bald head to be called Cupid ... Well, it's a bit vertical, as you might say.

TERRY: (*Puzzled*) Vertical?

CUPID: Steep, miss ...

TERRY: (*Smiling*) I see. Well, what would you like to be called?

CUPID: If it's all the same to you, miss, I've got a fancy for Sydney. Not Syd – Sydney with a Y.

TERRY: It's all the same to me, Cupid ... er ... Sydney.

CUPID: Thank you, miss. An' I only 'ope the distinguished guests who patronise this sophisticated hostel will emulate your democratic touch of familiarity. (*Briskly*) One dry Martini!

TERRY: Thank you. Well ... here's luck, Sydney!

CUPID: Thank you, Miss Slade.

There is a pause.

TERRY: (*Quietly*) Who's that tall man? No, over on the other side, near the table ... Yes, that's right!

CUPID:	That's Mr Shackleton, miss. Arthur Shackleton.
TERRY:	Why, yes, of course. He doesn't look very happy, does he?
CUPID:	No, now you come to mention is, miss, he certainly doesn't. Looks distinctly miserable in fact. (*Almost as an afterthought*) He's a playwright.
TERRY:	Maybe that accounts for it.
CUPID:	I expect you'll be glad to get away from all this, miss. Often thought how fed up you girls must get ... dancing around every blinkin' night.
TERRY:	You ... sort of ... get used to it.
CUPID:	Yes, I suppose you do. (*Brightly*) Still, marriage is the only career for a young lady ... that's what I always says ...
TERRY:	Is it, Sydney?
CUPID:	Providing o' course there's lots of L.S.D. ... Love in a cottage is all very well if the cottage 'as got central heating an' the things you've been used to ... that's what I always says.
TERRY:	Is it, Sydney?
CUPID:	And how is Mr Swift ...? Can't say I've seen 'im about lately.
TERRY:	Oh, he's not too bad ... considering.
CUPID:	Decided on a date, miss?
TERRY:	(*After a tiny pause*) Sydney, I think perhaps it's only fair to tell you. Peter and I have decided to ... call the whole thing off.
CUPID:	(*Amazed*) What do you mean ... Call the whole thing off ...?
TERRY:	(*Obviously distressed*) It's really quite an old story. There's nothing very new about it. His father happens to be the director of a bank ... a

	very large bank … Oh, such an important bank, Sydney!
CUPID:	I get it, miss. The old musical comedy angle. Dance hostess not good enough for wealthy young playboy … Millionaire father intervenes. Blimey, I thought that went out with the crystal set!
TERRY:	Apparently it didn't …
CUPID:	But … what's going to happen?
TERRY:	I'm staying on here, for the time being at any rate.
CUPID:	Well, I'm sorry, miss.
TERRY:	It's not exactly what I had in mind … still, we've had some marvellous times together – Peter and I, and … and they can't take that away from me.

TERRY sings They Can't Take That Away From Me.

CUPID:	Well, it's no good getting down hearted, miss. Love's a peculiar thing – and I'm speaking from experience too, miss – if you'll permit me to say so!
TERRY:	Experience, Cupid?
CUPID:	(*Softly*) Sydney …
TERRY:	I beg your pardon … Sydney.
CUPID:	Yes, miss – experience. I've been married fourteen years and I've still a lot to learn. Mind you, I'm not complaining! Don't get the wrong impression – I'm not complaining!
TERRY:	Fourteen years – I'd no idea you'd been married as long as that.
CUPID:	Yes, miss – fourteen years. Effie and me was married at two-thirty on Easter Monday, Nineteen-twenty-nine! Blimey, it makes me sound like a museum piece, don't it?

TERRY:	(*Laughing*) I expect you took to married life like a duck to water.
CUPID:	Oh, no! Oh, no … not the first year, miss. By jingo, no! Too many peculiar things 'appened. (*Hastily*) Don't get me wrong: By peculiar, I don't mean funny in the sense of being peculiar, I mean peculiar in the sense of …
TERRY:	(*Laughing*) You mean Peculiar!
CUPID:	That's right, miss. (*Confidentially*) You see, in my young days I'd always been a bit of a spark, so …
TERRY:	(*Playfully shocked*) A bit of a spark, Sydney?
CUPID:	Well, I 'ad my moments and I'd made the most of them, as you might say – so when I first got married, I felt a little like …
TERRY:	Bluebeard!
CUPID:	Oh, no, miss – not Bluebeard! Like Jeremiah Jones.
TERRY:	Jeremiah Jones?
CUPID:	Yes – now don't tell me you've never heard of Jeremiah Jones!

CUPID sings Hello, Hello, Who's Your Lady Friend?
ARTHUR SHACKLETON arrives at the cocktail bar.

ARTHUR:	Good evening, Cupid.
CUPID:	Good evening, Mr Shackleton. Glass of sherry, sir?
ARTHUR:	I think I'd rather like … er … a Bronx.
CUPID:	We've got a very nice sherry, sir …
ARTHUR:	Yes … I will have a Bronx.
CUPID:	One Bronx …
TERRY:	And a dry Martini, <u>Sydney</u>.
CUPID:	Thank <u>you</u>, Miss Slade.

A tiny pause.

| ARTHUR: | Hotel seems pretty crowded … |

TERRY: Very.

ARTHUR: Cigarette?

TERRY: No thank you.

ARTHUR: Haven't we met before somewhere?

TERRY: I don't think so.

ARTHUR: Odd, I don't usually forget a face.

TERRY: That must be very comforting.

CUPID: One Bronx ... one dry Martini.

TERRY: Thank you, Sydney.

ARTHUR: Why do you call him Sydney? His name's Cupid.

TERRY: He prefers Sydney.

ARTHUR: Why?

TERRY: Wouldn't you ... if your name was Cupid?

ARTHUR: (*Amused*) Possibly. (*After a tiny pause*) You know, we have met somewhere before, I'm quite sure. Ah, I've got it! Lady Tracey's ... you wore a white dress, blue sandals ... and danced all the night with Peter Swift.

TERRY: Yes. Yes, that's right! (*Pleased*) Fancy you remembering ...

ARTHUR: I told you, I never forget a face. Especially if it happens to be a happy one.

TERRY: A happy one ...?

ARTHUR: Yes. You looked divinely happy that night.

The orchestra commences to play.

TERRY: It was the night I met Peter ... for ... the first time.

ARTHUR: I see.

TERRY: Two months later we became engaged.

ARTHUR: Oh, well ... that explains it.

TERRY: Explains ... what ...?

ARTHUR: Explains why you managed to look so divinely happy at an excessively irritating party. It was really very dull, you know.

TERRY: (*Softly*) I can't remember anything about the party except ... that ... for me ... love walked right in ...

TERRY sings Love Walked Right In.

The orchestra continues.

ARTHUR: Do you often come here?

TERRY: I work here. I'm kind of ... a dance hostess ... (*Bitterly*) ... or gigolette, if you prefer it.

ARTHUR: I prefer it. (*To CUPID*) I'm not very keen on this Bronx. I think I'll have ...

CUPID: (*Hopefully*) We've got a very nice sherry, sir.

ARTHUR: I think I'll have a Gin and Italian.

CUPID: (*Disappointed*) Yes, sir. Very good, sir.

The orchestra stops.

ARTHUR: Won't you join me?

TERRY: No thank you.

ARTHUR: (*Casually*) What made your fiancé ... call things off ...? (*Calling*) Just a spot of Italian, Cupid!

CUPID: (*In the background*) Yes, sir.

TERRY: (*Softly*) How did ... you know my engagement had been broken?

ARTHUR: You haven't answered my question.

A tiny pause.

TERRY: It's not a very interesting story ...

ARTHUR: Why do women always say that? It's not a very interesting story.

TERRY: I'm afraid I'm not feeling in a very auto-biographical mood, Mr Shackleton ... Supposing you tell me the story of *your* life?

ARTHUR: My life? (*He laughs*) Oh ... oh, now you've started something.

TERRY: Have you ever been in love?

ARTHUR: Once. But let's start at the beginning, shall we? I wrote a play. A very good play. And I made a lot of money, Miss Slade. Oh, such a lot of money! (*Quietly*) I saw the world. I saw places I'd always wanted to see. Strange little out of the way places, each steeped in their own peculiar perfume of life. I went everywhere and I saw everything. I met a great many people ... a great many distinguished people ... a great many women. But there was only one woman I really cared for ... and she was very lovely. Last night I met her for the second time and I asked her to be my wife.

TERRY: She ... disappointed you?

ARTHUR: Do I look like a man who is supremely happy?

TERRY: I'm afraid not.

CUPID: One Gin and Italian sir.

The orchestra starts to play again.

ARTHUR: Thank you.

ARTHUR drinks.

There is a pause.

TERRY: What are you going to do now?

ARTHUR: We both seem to be in the same boat, don't we?

TERRY: Yes.

ARTHUR: So far as I can see there's only one thing we can do ... Let's face the music and dance!

ARTHUR sings Let's Face The Music.

ARTHUR: How about another drink?

TERRY: I'd rather not if you don't mind.

ARTHUR: I think I'll ... er ...

CUPID: Did I recommend the sherry, sir?

ARTHUR: ... I'll ... er ... have another Gin and Italian.

CUPID: (*Wearily*) Very good, sir.

The telephone rings.

CUPID: (*On the phone*) Hello? … Yes, speaking … Yes, hold on … Hold on, Mr Swift! (*Excitedly: to TERRY*) It's for you, miss! Take it in the box over there!

TERRY: (*Delighted*) Oh … Oh, thank you!

A pause.

A telephone receiver is lifted.

TERRY: Hello? … Hello? … Why, yes, Peter … Yes … yes … Yes, darling … (*Softly*) Not over the phone … You – you know how much, Peter … Yes … Yes … Yes, darling … always.

TERRY sings My Heart and I.

The orchestra continues.

TERRY: (*Still on the phone*) Yes – all right, darling. Goodbye.

TERRY rings off.

A pause.

CUPID: (*Anxiously*) Is … is everything all right, miss?

TERRY: (*Quickly*) Everything's … all right, Sydney.

CUPID: I am glad, miss! Blimey … I am glad.

TERRY: (*Laughing*) Thank you, Sydney. You're a darling.

CUPID: Your Gin and Italian, sir.

ARTHUR: Thank you. I drink to your future, Miss Slade. And to the gentleman who has had the good sense to change his mind.

TERRY: It was never Peter's fault that we parted … I always knew that. (*Brightly*) See you later, Cupid! Goodnight, Mr Shackleton!

ARTHUR: Goodnight!

CUPID: Goodnight, miss.

A pause.

ARTHUR: You look positively brimming over with high spirits.

CUPID: I feel it, sir. There's nothing I like better than an 'appy ending. (*Suddenly*) I'm sorry about your packet o' trouble, sir.

ARTHUR: My packet o' trouble, Cupid?

CUPID: Your young lady turning you down, sir.

ARTHUR: Oh, but she didn't turn me down, Cupid.

CUPID: She … she didn't turn you down?

ARTHUR: No.

CUPID: Then why the 'ell are you feeling so miserable? (*Brightly*) You'll be settling down, Mr Shackleton. A nice little house near …

ARTHUR: (*Quietly*) I saw the world. I saw places I'd always wanted to see. Strange little out of the way places, each steeped in their own peculiar perfume of life … I don't suppose I shall ever see them again … now.

CUPID: I understand, Mr Shackleton. I understand. (*Gently*) But you'll get used to it …

ARTHUR: Like being called Cupid?

CUPID: That's right, sir. Like being called Cupid. (*Pleasantly*) Another dry Martini, Mr Shackleton?

ARTHUR: I think I'll have a sherry, Sydney.

The orchestra commences to play These Foolish Things.

THE END

WE WERE STRANGERS

A ONE ACT PLAY
FOR THE STAGE

CHARACTERS:
NICHOLAS FORBES
GAIL BLAKE
HOBSON

This stage play was written in 1937, and was not produced professionally but released to amateurs in 1948. It became a radio play, broadcast on 3 June 1938 with Hugh Morton as Nicholas, Hilary Williams as Gail and William Hughes as Hobson

A new production was broadcast on 9 July 1940 with D.A. Clarke-Smith as Nicholas, Pauline Vilda as Gail and Philip Wade as Hobson

Another new production was broadcast on 16 September 1941 with Carl Bernard as Nicholas,

Grizelda Hervey as Gail and Antony Holles as Hobson

SCENE: A small jeweller's shop in New Bond Street
TIME: The present, Saturday morning

The scene is the interior of a small jeweller's shop in New Bond Street. A door leading to the street is up centre, and another door leading to a private office is down right.

Above the door is a small counter, on which there are numerous glass trays containing watches, statuettes, rings, etc. Behind this counter, and right of the entrance, are green curtains concealing a long, low window. Two chairs are facing the counter

When the curtain rises HOBSON is discovered behind the counter, carefully examining a tray of rings. He is a spruce little man of about forty-five.

NICHOLAS FORBES enters from the street. He is tall and good looking.

HOBSON: Good morning, sir!
NICHOLAS: Good morning. I want to see Mr Stanford, please.
HOBSON: I'm rather afraid Mr Stanford is out at the moment, sir. Anything I can do for you?
NICHOLAS: Well, I don't see why not. I should like to see some engagement rings.
HOBSON: Yes, of course, sir.
HOBSON places a tray of rings on a small black cloth.
NICHOLAS: (*Examining a ring*) I rather like this one.
HOBSON: That's a lovely little ring, sir, and a genuine bargain. Thirty-six guineas.
NICHOLAS: (*Smiling*) Oh, I see. Well, as a matter of fact, I want something rather more expensive.
HOBSON: Rather more expensive? (*Taking a ring from another tray*) Well, how does this strike you, sir?

NICHOLAS:	No. No, I'm afraid I don't care for that sort of thing.
HOBSON:	A little too ostentatious, eh, sir?
NICHOLAS:	Yes, a little too – er – ostentatious. (*Examining a third ring*) This is rather charming.
HOBSON:	A hundred and seven guineas, sir.
NICHOLAS:	A hundred and seven? Rather a big jump from thirty-six.
HOBSON:	Yes, sir. But the stone in this ring, apart from being larger is definitely of –
NICHOLAS:	(*Thoughtfully*) Mm – I can't say I'm really keen on it. Have you anything a little more – er – exclusive?
HOBSON:	Exclusive? About what price have you in mind, sir?
NICHOLAS:	Oh. Two-fifty. Three hundred.
HOBSON:	Oh, I see. (*Dubiously*) I – don't – think – we have, sir. (*Suddenly*) But I'm expecting Mr Stanford back at any moment, and I rather think he may have something that might –
NICHOLAS:	About how long do you think Mr Stanford will be?
HOBSON:	At the very most ten minutes, sir.
NICHOLAS:	Then, if you don't mind, I'll wait.
HOBSON:	(*Pleased*) Certainly, sir.

NICHOLAS sits.

NICHOLAS:	(*Making conversation*) Are you busy?
HOBSON:	Fairly busy, sir. We have our moments like every one else.
NICHOLAS:	I see.
HOBSON:	Excuse my asking, sir. But aren't you Mr Forbes – Mr Nicholas Forbes, the explorer?
NICHOLAS:	Yes.

HOBSON:	(*Rather thrilled*) I thought I recognized you.
NICHOLAS:	(*Politely*) Have we met before, then?
HOBSON:	Oh, no, sir. But I saw your film Heroes of the Jungle.
NICHOLAS:	(*Rather bored*) Oh.
HOBSON:	A very fine film if I may say so, sir.
NICHOLAS:	Thank you.
HOBSON:	I took my little boy to see it and he was very thrilled – very thrilled indeed.
NICHOLAS:	That's most gratifying.
HOBSON:	(*Very interested*) Personally, I could never understand how you managed to escape from that lion, sir. The one that entered your tent.
NICHOLAS:	It was a very old lion, Mr –?
HOBSON:	Hobson.
NICHOLAS:	Mr Hobson.
HOBSON:	Oh. (*Puzzled*) Oh, I see.

GAIL BLAKE enters. She is a very lovely looking woman of about thirty-five. Exquisitely dressed. At the moment she is the victim of a violent, and rather embarrassing, attack of hiccups.

NICHOLAS rises.

GAIL:	Good – *hic* – morning.
HOBSON:	Good morning, madam.

GAIL produces a small oval-shaped box, obviously containing a ring.

GAIL:	About two days ago my fiancé purchased this engagement ring, and …
HOBSON:	Oh, yes, of course. I remember, madam. In fact, I believe I attended to the gentleman personally.
GAIL:	He said that if I didn't care for it you'd be quite willing to – *hic* – to – *hic* – exchange it?
HOBSON:	Why, yes, of course, madam.

69

GAIL:	(*Sweetly*) Well, I'm afraid I don't – er – care for it.
HOBSON:	I see. Then we'll exchange it, by all means. Have you the receipt?
GAIL:	(*Searching in her handbag*) Yes, it's – *hic* – it's – *hic* – *hic*. (*Irritably*) Really, I beg your pardon, but I've had these confounded hiccups all the morning.
HOBSON:	Can I get you a glass of water, madam?
GAIL:	I'm afraid it – *hic* – *hic* – it wouldn't be any use, you see –
NICHOLAS:	(*Very calmly*) Hold your breath and count sixteen.
GAIL:	(*Rather indignantly*) I beg your – *hic* – pardon?
NICHOLAS:	I said: Hold your breath and count sixteen.
GAIL:	(*Coldly*) I've already held my breath and counted thirty-nine. I fail to see –
NICHOLAS:	(*Excessively polite*) Sixteen makes all the difference.
HOBSON:	(*Apologetically*) This is – is Mr Forbes, madam. The – er – famous explorer.
GAIL:	Really. Do explorers suffer from hiccups?
NICHOLAS:	Not for any length of time, they always –
GAIL:	Hold their breath and count sixteen, I suppose?
NICHOLAS:	Precisely.
GAIL:	(*After a tiny pause*) Very well. (*She holds her breath. A long pause*) Ah!
NICHOLAS:	Well?
GAIL:	(*Coldly*) It doesn't seem to have made the slightest difference.
HOBSON:	(*Tactfully*) About the – er – receipt, madam?

GAIL: Oh, yes – the receipt. Where did I … Oh, here we are! (*She takes a slip of paper from her handbag*)

HOBSON: Thank you, madam. Now will you excuse me, please? I'm afraid I shall have to check the number in our books. Mr Stanford always insists on this. It shouldn't take very long.

GAIL: That's quite all right.

HOBSON goes into the private office.

There is a pause.

NICHOLAS: Do you often suffer from hiccups?

GAIL: I've never had them in my life before.

NICHOLAS: Oh. (*Pause*) I once knew a man who had hiccups for three days.

GAIL: Really.

NICHOLAS: Yes. (*A tiny pause*) On the third day he took a cold bath. It cured him completely.

GAIL: I'm so glad.

NICHOLAS: It was a great relief.

GAIL: I'm sure it must have been.

NICHOLAS: (*As an afterthought*) Unfortunately, he caught a chill and died of pneumonia.

GAIL: Oh.

A pause.

NICHOLAS: Do you know, I feel quite sure that we've met before somewhere.

GAIL: I feel quite sure that we haven't.

NICHOLAS: I never forget a face.

GAIL: Neither do I.

NICHOLAS: (*Attempting to pursue the conversation*) Tell me, do you find it an advantage or a disadvantage?

GAIL: (*Puzzled*) What?

NICHOLAS: Never being able to forget faces?

71

GAIL: (*Curtly*) I've never thought about it.

A pause.

NICHOLAS: (*Suddenly bright*) I once knew a man who could never forget feet.

GAIL: You seem to have a large circle of rather unique acquaintances.

NICHOLAS: (*Magnanimously*) Really, you know, in exploration one meets so many people. It's rather inevitable.

GAIL: I seem to remember reading something about you in The Tatler. Didn't you go to the North Pole or somewhere?

NICHOLAS: It was the North Pole.

GAIL: (*Sweetly*) I hope you enjoyed it.

NICHOLAS: Thank you. It was very pleasant.

GAIL: (*Puzzled*) I've often wondered. Why do people go to the North Pole?

NICHOLAS: (*After a pause – equally puzzled*) I haven't the faintest idea.

GAIL: Exploring always seem to me rather a mug's game. I can see very little point in dashing from one place to another when it's far more comfortable staying where you are.

NICHOLAS: I can see you've given the subject a great deal of thought.

GAIL: Didn't you once make a film – Heroes of the Jungle?

NICHOLAS: Yes.

GAIL: I saw it in Brighton about two years ago. I loved the part where you were chased by that decrepit old lion.

NICHOLAS: Thank you.

GAIL: Did you ever see it?

NICHOLAS:	Once. Now I come to think about it – that's why I went to the North Pole.
GAIL:	(*Amused*) Oh, I see.
NICHOLAS:	(*Seriously*) When you smile like that – I can't help thinking you remind me of someone. Are you sure we haven't met before?
GAIL:	Quite sure.
NICHOLAS:	It's rather odd that …
GAIL:	Did you ever see a play at the Lyric called Captain Denby's Excuse? It ran for almost a year.
NICHOLAS:	Captain Denby's Excuse? Why, yes. (*Suddenly*) Good Lord, of course! I remember – you played the excuse. You're – you're Gail Blake. Gail Blake, the actress.
GAIL:	(*Quietly amused*) Yes. Yes, that's right.
NICHOLAS:	(*After a tiny pause*) You were – awfully good.
GAIL:	Did you really think so?
NICHOLAS:	(*Slowly*) Terribly – good. (*A slight pause*) I say, I hope you don't mind my saying so?
GAIL:	(*Inwardly delighted*) No. No, of course not.
NICHOLAS:	I saw the play four times.
GAIL:	Really?
NICHOLAS:	I shall never forget that last act. You wore a blue dress. Blue sequins, wasn't it?
GAIL:	How perfectly sweet of you to remember! (*A tiny pause*) I got awfully good notices.
NICHOLAS:	I'm sure you did.
GAIL:	James Agate said the sweetest things – all in French, too. Much more intriguing, don't you think?
NICHOLAS:	Much more intriguing.
GAIL:	(*Very friendly*) Are you very interested in the theatre, Mr –?

NICHOLAS: Forbes. Nicholas Forbes.

GAIL: Oh, yes, of course. Mr Forbes …?

NICHOLAS: Very interested.

GAIL: My fiancé's an actor, too. You've probably heard of him – Brian Steele?

NICHOLAS: Brian Steele? Yes, I've heard of him – of course. But didn't he sail for America yesterday?

GAIL: He's gone to Hollywood. I'm joining him in New York at Christmas. We're to be married there.

NICHOLAS: Oh, I see. Congratulations.

GAIL: Thank you. (*After a tiny pause*) I'm rather looking forward to it. I've never been to New York.

NICHOLAS: I'm to be married at Christmas, too, oddly enough. I'm joining my fiancée in Scotland.

GAIL: Really? Congratulations.

NICHOLAS: Thank you. (*After a tiny pause*) I'm rather looking forward to it. I've never been to Scotland.

GAIL: They say it's charming.

NICHOLAS: Yes.

A pause.

GAIL: Very hilly.

A pause.

NICHOLAS: Oh, very.

GAIL: Have you – known your fiancée very long?

NICHOLAS: About two months. We met at a party. A coming-out party. She was coming out just as I was arriving. We bumped.

GAIL: I see.

NICHOLAS: And – Brian?

| GAIL: | Brian –? Oh, there's nothing much to tell, really. We first met in rep about six years ago. |
| NICHOLAS: | Oh. (*A tiny pause*) Mr Hobson seems to be taking his time. I should sit down if I were you. |

GAIL sits.
A pause.

GAIL:	Please forgive me for my rudeness just now.
NICHOLAS:	Rudeness?
GAIL:	Yes. I ought to have thanked you for curing my hiccups.
NICHOLAS:	Oh, that was nothing.
GAIL:	But I was so unnecessarily irritable, please …
NICHOLAS:	Nonsense! You had every right to be irritable. Besides, there's nothing more aggravating than a gust of hiccups.
GAIL:	You're very sweet.
NICHOLAS:	Not at all.
GAIL:	I must remember that trick about counting sixteen. It's extremely useful.
NICHOLAS:	Yes. It only has one disadvantage. It doesn't always work.
GAIL:	(*Amused*) I see.

A slight pause.

NICHOLAS:	(*Offering his cigarette case*) Cigarette?
GAIL:	No, thank you.
NICHOLAS:	You don't mind if I smoke?
GAIL:	No. No, of course not.

NICHOLAS lights his cigarette.

| NICHOLAS: | So you're exchanging your engagement ring? |
| GAIL: | Well, I hope to do so. It isn't very charming, is it? |

GAIL shows NICHOLAS her engagement ring.

GAIL:	Brian has simply no taste – in jewellery, I mean.
NICHOLAS:	It is a little – er – ostentatious, if I may quote Mr Hobson.
GAIL:	And you?
NICHOLAS:	Me? Well, as a matter of fact, I'm waiting to see Mr Stafford – the proprietor here.
GAIL:	Is he a friend of yours?
NICHOLAS:	Not really a friend. A sort of acquaintance. We met in Los Angeles about two years ago.
GAIL:	(*Briskly*) Los Angeles? Oh, isn't that near Hollywood?
NICHOLAS:	(*Amused*) Yes, quite near, I believe.

A pause.

GAIL:	I suppose you'll be spending your honeymoon in Scotland?
NICHOLAS:	More than likely.
GAIL:	What part?
NICHOLAS:	I don't really know. Maybe the Highlands. Beatrice seems very keen on the Highlands.
GAIL:	Beatrice …?
NICHOLAS:	Yes.
GAIL:	I have a sister called Beatrice.
NICHOLAS:	It's not a name I really care for.
GAIL:	(*A shade embarrassed*) Well – I rather like Bea.
NICHOLAS:	(*Pensively*) No one calls her Bea.
GAIL:	Oh. (*After a tiny pause*) Is she fair?
NICHOLAS:	(*Quietly, almost mechanically*) She's tall and dark, with very beautiful eyes, and every one calls her Beatrice.
GAIL:	Oh. (*With a little laugh*) Oh, I see.
NICHOLAS:	(*Quietly*) I wonder if you do see, Miss – (*Suddenly*) May I call you Gail?

GAIL: Well –

NICHOLAS: (*Gently*) Please?

GAIL: If it will afford you any pleasure – yes. Personally, I derive very little delight from calling comparative strangers by their Christian names.

NICHOLAS: So do I. But this is different. Much different.

GAIL: Is it?

NICHOLAS: (*Looking at GAIL very intently*) Yes. you see, we're not strangers, Gail. At least, not any longer.

GAIL: Then what are we?

A pause.

NICHOLAS: We are in love.

A tiny pause.

GAIL: (*Quietly*) I beg your pardon?

NICHOLAS: We are in love. Deeply in love.

GAIL: (*Annoyed*) Please, don't be silly!

NICHOLAS: I'm not being silly, Gail. Don't think that. I'm being sincere – desperately sincere.

GAIL: You're talking complete nonsense!

NICHOLAS: You're not annoyed?

GAIL: (*Stiffly*) I have no wish to pursue the subject.

NICHOLAS: From the very first moment when you came into this shop – something happened. I don't know what it was. I don't pretend to know. But deep down inside of me a devotion stirred – a devotion that I have never felt for anyone or anything in my life before.

GAIL: (*Slightly alarmed*) But – but you know nothing about me.

NICHOLAS: Is that so important? I don't see that it's going to help me any if I know what you look like at

	half-past eight in a morning, or what sort of face powder your sister uses.
GAIL:	(*Sharply*) You're infatuated. Stupidly and childishly infatuated.
NICHOLAS:	(*Quietly*) That's a very silly observation, and not worthy of you, my dearest.
GAIL:	Please – please go away!
NICHOLAS:	Why are you behaving like this? It's not a bit kind and it's very unintelligent.
GAIL:	Unintelligent!
NICHOLAS:	Very.
GAIL:	Well – perhaps you'll be kind enough to tell me precisely what you expect of me? Would a girlish swoon satisfy your apparently modest requirements?
NICHOLAS:	While being equally unintelligent, that at least would be a far more romantic procedure.
GAIL:	I simply don't know how you have the audacity to stand there and talk such utter nonsense about being in love. How can you possibly be in love?
NICHOLAS:	(*Gently*) You're very lovely.
GAIL:	And it's no good trying to flatter me, because I'm quite immune to flattery.
NICHOLAS:	(*Politely*) I'm sure you are.
GAIL:	I think your behaviour is perfectly ungentlemanly.
NICHOLAS:	Ungentlemanly? I'm sorry. (*Taking GAIL by the arm*) Now would you mind terribly if I asked you a question?
GAIL:	(*After a tiny pause*) Well?
NICHOLAS:	Despite this antagonistic attitude of yours – you do believe me, don't you?
GAIL:	What do you mean?

78

NICHOLAS: You do believe that this thing has happened.
              That we are in love. Deeply in love?

GAIL: I certainly do not.

NICHOLAS: (*Fervently*) Then why are your lips trembling,
              my dear, and your eyes shining with a soft
              light?

GAIL: If you don't stop talking such nonsense I shall
              – I shall … (*She falters*)

NICHOLAS: (*Gently*) My dear, don't you see – it's no use?
              This is a moment in a million. An enchanted
              moment. A moment that means more to both
              of us than either the past or the future. It
              won't last. It can't last. But while it does, my
              sweet, don't let's waste it with hollow little
              phrases and conventional emotions.

GAIL: (*Softly*) Leave go of my arm – please.

A slight pause.

NICHOLAS: All right. All right, if you insist.

NICHOLAS lets GAIL's arm drop and half turns away.

GAIL: Thank you.

A pause.

Suddenly, NICHOLAS turns towards GAIL again.

NICHOLAS: Forgive me if I've annoyed you. If I've
              seemed just a little mad and impetuous, but –

GAIL: (*Gently*) I'm not annoyed.

NICHOLAS: I'm sorry, too, if all this has hurt you a little.
              The suddenness of it, I mean. But – but we
              are in love. Aren't we? (*A pause*) Aren't we?

GAIL: (*Slowly*) Yes.

NICHOLAS: This isn't just love at first sight. Don't think
              that. Please don't think that. It's much more
              important. Much more enchanting. (*Suddenly*)
              Why are you smiling?

GAIL:	(*Amused*) I was just thinking. This moment has its funny points. It really has. I came here to exchange my engagement ring, and you – you came here to buy one.
NICHOLAS:	(*Laughing*) Yes.
GAIL:	(*Seriously*) And have you, even once, thought of Beatrice?
NICHOLAS:	(*Vehemently*) Damn Beatrice!
GAIL:	I'm sure that's a little unfair.
NICHOLAS:	Yes. I'm sorry.

A tiny pause.

GAIL:	What's going to happen?
NICHOLAS:	I don't know. (*After a tiny pause*) You said your – your fiancé was in America?
GAIL:	Yes.
NICHOLAS:	And mine's in Scotland.
GAIL:	Yes.
NICHOLAS:	I can't quite make up my mind whether that's an advantage or a disadvantage.
GAIL:	I'm not sure either.
NICHOLAS:	We could write.
GAIL:	Yes. (*A slight pause*) Yes, but we're not going to.
NICHOLAS:	Why not?
GAIL:	Have you forgotten what you said just now? About us? About this moment? You said: "It won't last. It can't last."
NICHOLAS:	(*Fiercely*) That's ridiculous. I didn't mean it. It slipped out. It's got to last, Gail! It's got to last!
GAIL:	Yes, but it won't. (*Slowly and rather puzzled*) I've never felt like this in my life before, and – I can't understand it. I know the situation's impossible, fantastic, and – and ludicrous. I

know that judged from certain standards it's even degrading. But this second nothing seems real beyond the fact that – I love you. Beyond the fact that I want you always to remember and believe – I love you.

NICHOLAS: Thank you, my dear. (*A pause*) Gail …

GAIL: Yes?

NICHOLAS: I have a small place in Sussex. I was going down there for the weekend. Perhaps if you came we might, together, find a solution to our problem.

GAIL: It's no good us trying to find a solution; because we haven't got a problem. This isn't a problem, my dear – and you know it isn't. It's just a moment. A complete moment of strange enchantment that belongs to both of us. There's nothing certain or real about it, beyond the fact that – it won't last. (*After a pause. Softly*) In a very short while you'll be thinking of Scotland and Beatrice again, and I shall be thinking of Brian and New York.

NICHOLAS: No. You know that's not true!

GAIL: And you know, only too well, that it is.

A pause.

NICHOLAS: Well?

GAIL: (*Softly*) I'm going.

GAIL turns towards the door.

NICHOLAS: Going!

GAIL: Yes. I've no wish to be here when this moment fades – when the enchantment vanishes.

NICHOLAS: (*Suddenly crossing towards GAIL*) Gail, please! Listen! Listen before you –

GAIL: No, don't follow me – please don't. Please
                   don't. (*Gently*) Just hold your breath, dearest
                   heart, and count sixteen.

GAIL goes out.

NICHOLAS goes rather hesitatingly towards the door.

He stops.

After a long pause HOBSON returns from the private office.

HOBSON: (*Apologetically*) Really, I'm terribly sorry to
                   … (*He notices that GAIL is no longer
                   present*) Oh! The lady's gone, sir!

NICHOLAS: (*Very softly*) Yes.

HOBSON: I thought she wanted to exchange her
                   engagement ring?

A slight pause.

NICHOLAS returns to the counter.

NICHOLAS: (*Quietly*) She did. But she changed her mind,
                   instead.

HOBSON: (*Puzzled*) Oh. Oh, I see. (*After a tiny pause*)
                   Did the young lady say whether she was
                   coming back or not, sir?

NICHOLAS: No. But I'm desperately afraid that she isn't,
                   Mr Hobson.

HOBSON: Oh.

NICHOLAS: I've decided not to wait for Mr Stanford, I'll –

HOBSON: I'm very sorry, sir. Mr Stanford said he would
                   definitely be back by eleven-thirty.

NICHOLAS: That's all right. As a matter of fact, I've
                   already reached a decision about the ring.
                   (*Taking a ring from one of the glass trays*) I'll
                   take this one.

HOBSON: Thank you, sir. (*Surprised*) Oh! But sir …

NICHOLAS: (*Quietly*) What's the matter?

HOBSON: (*Amused*) Well – this is the first ring I showed
                   you.

82

NICHOLAS: Yes. Yes, I know.

HOBSON: (*Bewildered*) But – but it's only thirty-six guineas, sir!

NICHOLAS: (*With a sigh*) It will do, Mr Hobson. It will do.

NICHOLAS extracts his wallet.

THE CURTAIN FALLS

MARY ANN
Broadcast on BBC Radio
29th April 1935
in the concert party programme *The Air-Do-Wells*

A new production of this sketch was included in *Jack Payne's Radio Party*, broadcast on 30 November 1935

Another new production was included in *Just Fancy That!* broadcast on 8 January 1937

GEORGE: It's a rum life, Maggie.

MAGGIE: Aye! It's a rum life, Garge,

GEORGE: All 'ustle and bustle, Maggie.

MAGGIE: Aye! All 'ustle and bustle, Garge.

GEORGE: Nowt to do from o' getting up till time o' going to bed, Maggie.

MAGGIE: (*Decisively*) Nowt, Garge.

GEORGE: (*Rising*) Well, I reckon I'll have to be getting along. Times o'flitting.

MAGGIE: It's lonely here o' night, Garge.

GEORGE: Aye, Maggie! It's a pity ye daughter ain't 'ere, she'd 'ave been grand company for ye these lonely nights.

MAGGIE: (*With a sigh*) Poor Mary Ann!

GEORGE: (*Curious*) What happened to Mary Ann, oftens the time I used to see her playing around this cottage?

MAGGIE: It's a strange story, Garge. A strange story. Fourteen year ago come last Michaelmas I sent poor little Mary Ann down into the village. To the draper's, Garge, to buy me a pair of suspenders. Yes, a pair of suspenders it were. I waited and waited for her return, Garge, but I've never so much as clapped eyes on her since.

GEORGE: (*Sad*) I'm right sorry, Maggie.

MAGGIE: (*With a sigh*) Ah well, what has been will be, and what isn't won't!

GEORGE: Aye, ye're right!

MAGGIE: Good night, Garge.

GEORGE: Bless ye, Maggie.

MAGGIE: And give my love to Mrs Lovat.

GEORGE: (*Suddenly surprised*) Why bless me soul, 'ere's a stranger coming up the path!

MAGGIE: A stranger this time o' night!

GEORGE: Aye, and a mighty pretty 'en too.

The door opens.

MAGGIE: What be ye wanting here, miss, this time o' night?

GIRL: (*Excited*) Mother! Mother! Don't you recognise me? I'm Mary Ann, Mother! Your little Mary Ann. Fourteen years ago, Mother, you sent me down into the village for a pair of suspenders. I ran away from home, Mother. I went on the stage. I worked and worked and worked. (*Excited*) At last came my big chance! I made good, Mother. Your little Mary Ann was a success! I'm the sensation of New York! The riot of Paris, and the darling of London! People all over the world are speaking of my fame. (*Sweetly*) And now, now I have returned home. Mother, what have you to say?

MAGGIE: Where the hell's my suspenders?

THE END

WORTH TAKING
Broadcast on BBC Radio
30th April 1936
in *Mr. Mike Presents*

A new production of this sketch was included in *Mr. Mike Presents*, broadcast on 27 July 1936

Another new production was included in *Just Fancy That!*, broadcast on 8 January 1937

Another new production was included in *The Time of March*, broadcast on 3 March 1937

ANNOUNCER: There seems to be a fashion these days for advertisements to tell a story. Well, at tremendous expense we have secured the broadcast rights of the new advertisement for Rowlands Fruit Syrup. This is in eight scenes and entitled How The Office Boy Pulled His Socks Up!

A door opens.

THOMAS: You sent for me, Mr Johnson?

JOHNSON: (*Angrily*) I did, Thomas! I did! I'm extremely tired of the way in which you are conducting yourself.

THOMAS: Oh, Mr Johnson?

JOHNSON: You are, without exception, the laziest and most incompetent office boy Johnson and Company have ever had. I give you just one week in which to pull your socks up!

THOMAS: (*Very depressed and weary*) Yes, Mr Johnson.

A pause.

ANNOUNCER: That night …

FADE IN a background of sentimental music.

FADE DOWN the music.

THOMAS: (*Depressed*) Johnson was on to me again, mummy.

MOTHER: Was he, my darling?

THOMAS: He says I'm lazy and incompetent. I'm not really lazy, it's just that I feel completely out of sorts and so, so terribly tired, mummy.

MOTHER: I should see a doctor, my dear. Why not go round to Dr Jenkins after supper?

THOMAS: Yes, I think I will.

A pause.

ANNOUNCER: At the doctor's …

DOCTOR: (*Pompously*) Day starvation, my boy, that's your trouble. You see, even when you're not in bed you're half asleep. Your energy is in fact just double what it should be if you were in bed and using half the energy you might otherwise use. Do I make my meaning clear?

THOMAS: Oh perfectly. And what do you recommend, doctor?

DOCTOR: Being a shareholder I naturally recommend Rowlands Fruit Syrup. A glass before, and after every meal. And, of course, a tankard with meals.

ANNOUNCER: Two months later …

FADE IN of snappy music.

FADE DOWN the music.

MOTHER: Are you still taking your Rowlands Fruit Syrup every night, Tommie?

THOMAS: (*Full of beans. Ridiculously healthy*) Rather, by George! It's simply spiffing, mater! Absolutely fills a chappie with health. Cheerio, mater, see you later. I'm just off to the Serpentine for a swim.

ANNOUNCER: Three months later …

FADE IN an orchestra playing Rule Britannia.

FADE DOWN the music.

JOHNSON: Ah, come in, Thomas!

THOMAS: (*Very brisky*) You sent me for me, Mr Johnson?

JOHNSON:	Thomas, I have some good news for you. Head Office have appointed you Assistant Manager to our Bombay Branch.
THOMAS:	But, sir, I am only an office boy!
JOHNSON:	No longer, Thomas! No longer! India, my boy! You sail on the 29th!
ANNOUNCER:	A month later …
MOTHER:	Have you packed your Rowlands Fruit Syrup, Tommie?
THOMAS:	Here it is, mother. Now don't worry. No harm can come to me while I have my fruit syrup.
MOTHER:	That's right, my darling. Always remember. Before, after, and during meals.
THOMAS:	And, of course, on retiring.
MOTHER:	That's right, my dear. Just enough to cover a half-crown.
ANNOUNCER:	(*Dramatically*) Three months later. An outpost of the Empire …

FADE IN Rule Britannia again.

FADE DOWN the music.

MAN:	By Gad, Gadsby, I don't know how that fellow Thomas can stick the pace. What a constitution! What a constitution!
2nd MAN:	Absolutely.
MAN:	He's never tired. Always as fresh as a daisy.
2nd MAN:	Absolutely.
MAN:	The bounder never touches whisky. Seems to wallow in some sort of fruit syrup. By Gad, if we don't pour his blasted fruit syrup down the sink he'll soon become Viceroy.
2nd MAN:	Absolutely!

FADE IN Rule Britannia again.

FADE DOWN the music.

ANNOUNCER: Twelve months later …

GIRL: The Managing Director would like to see you, Mr Johnson.

JOHNSON: The new fellow, eh? Oh, well – here goes …

A door opens.

JOHNSON: You sent for me, Sir Thomas?

THOMAS: (*Angrily*) I did, Johnson! I did! I'm extremely tired of the way in which you are conducting yourself.

JOHNSON: Oh?

THOMAS: You are, without exception, the laziest and most incompetent manager Johnson and Company have ever had. I give you just one week in which to pull your socks up!

THE END

EXCUSES
Broadcast on BBC Radio
2nd June 1936
in *Mr. Mike Presents*

A new production of this sketch was included in *Variety in Miniature*, broadcast on 19 January 1937

Another new production was included in *Everything Stops for Tea*, broadcast on 25 September 1939

HUSBAND:	(*Nervously*) Good morning, my dear.
WIFE:	Good morning! (*Suddenly*) Henry!
HUSBAND:	Yes – er – my dear?
WIFE:	What time did you get in last night?
HUSBAND:	Er – twelve. No! Er – twelve-thirty – er – No! About – er – twelve!
WIFE:	Don't tell me you stayed at the office until that hour.
HUSBAND:	Yes dear. I mean – er – no dear.
WIFE:	Where <u>did</u> you get to?
HUSBAND:	The – er – club.
WIFE:	Well – what did you do at the club?
HUSBAND:	I – er – played bridge. No! Er – snooker – no – er billiards – er – er – whist!
WIFE:	Henry! What DID you do?
HUSBAND:	Well, we had a – er – sort of a general meeting.
WIFE:	Was the Chairman there?
HUSBAND:	Er – yes. Yes dear.
WIFE:	I see. Did *you* have anything to say at the meeting?
HUSBAND:	No. I – er – said nothing.
WIFE:	I suppose the Chairman did all the talking. Well – what did HE say?
HUSBAND:	As a matter of fact he offered – er – er – a silk hat to any member of the club who could stand up and truthfully say that during his married life he had never kissed any woman but his – er – er – wife. (*Laughing*) And no one stood up.
WIFE:	So no one stood up! And what was the matter with you, Henry Smythe?
HUSBAND:	Oh! Well I – er – had a sort of – well sort of …

WIFE: You had a sort of what? Now listen to me,
               worm. I'm not going to sit at this breakfast
               table morning after morning and be insulted.
               I've got some pride left, Henry Smythe. Some
               pride left from the days when dear mother
               used …

The voice FADES completely away…

COMPERE: And now for the same scene a week later. But
               this morning Henry has taken his first
               'Goodyarn' tablet.

A pause.
This scene is played rather swiftly.

WIFE: Good morning. (*Suddenly*) Henry!
HUSBAND: My dear?
WIFE: What time did you get home last night?
HUSBAND: Twelve-thirty-six my sweet. Greenwich mean
               time.
WIFE: Don't tell me you stayed at the office until
               that hour?
HUSBAND: Of course not. I went to the club.
WIFE: What did you do at the club?
HUSBAND: We had a general meeting.
WIFE: Was the Chairman there?
HUSBAND: Naturally.
WIFE: I see. Did you have anything to say at the
               meeting?
HUSBAND: Not a word.
WIFE: I suppose the Chairman did all the talking.
               Well – what did he say?
HUSBAND: He offered a silk hat to any member of the
               club who could stand up and truthfully say
               that during his married life he had never

kissed any woman but his wife. (*Amused*) And no one stood up.

WIFE: So no one stood up! And what was the matter with you, Henry Smythe?

HUSBAND: (*Briskly*) Darling! You know how damned silly I look in a silk hat!!!

THE END

THE KNAVE
Broadcast on BBC Radio
2nd June 1936
in *Mr. Mike Presents*

A new production of this sketch, read by Lionel Gamlin, was included in *Crime Magazine*, broadcast on 12 March 1940

Another new production was included in a twenty-minute programme with the story *Mark Conway Tells a Personal Tale of a Long Time Ago*, broadcast on 7 May 1940

Another new production, read by Godfrey Baseley and Martyn C. Webster, was included in *Words and Music*, broadcast on 8 September 1941

Another new production was included in the revue *Divertissement*, broadcast on 5 March 1943

MAN: Now, I'm not one of those fellows who believe everything they read in the newspapers. But nevertheless I did believe quite a lot about that person they called The Knave. He fascinated me. It seemed to me rather odd that a man should be able to impersonate people so perfectly that he could walk into their home or offices and do just what the devil he liked. The story of the Mayfair jewel robbery did more than fascinate me, it thrilled me. And it must have thrilled you too if you remember the case. The fellow – The Knave – apparently disguised himself as Lord Tenford, arrived at his Lordship's residence – was of course admitted – and calmly helped himself to several of Lady Tenford's proudest possessions. The butler <u>swore</u> it was Lord Tenford and several of the other servants corroborated his statement. But the fact remains, it was The Knave. The Knave in yet another of his masterly disguises. I was under the impression, like a great many other people, that for a man to be able to impersonate another man so that even that man's greatest friends would never recognise the deceit was impossible. And yet this appeared to be the sort of thing The Knave was doing day after day. I became a little sceptical. Perhaps after all the whole thing was considerably exaggerated by the newspapers. Then one week I bumped into a friend of mine. A fellow I hadn't seen for several months. He looked worried and dejected and – for a fellow who used to be one of the city's big noises – considerably down at heel. "Hello, Foster," I said cheerfully. "Looking a bit

103

despondent." He smiled. It was rather a weary smile. Then suddenly he said:

FOSTER: Yes – I've had a stroke of bad luck.

MAN: Sorry to hear it. Stock market been hitting you below the belt?

FOSTER: No. Nothing like that.

MAN: (*Jovially*) Don't tell me you've been falling for the gee-gees?

FOSTER: No. (*Seriously*) Derek, I'm … I'm cleared out. Broke. Completely broke.

MAN: (*Seriously*) Not really?

FOSTER: M'm.

MAN: As bad as that?

FOSTER: Fraid so.

MAN: But … but what's happened, Jim?

FOSTER: (*Quietly*) Ever heard of The Knave?

MAN: You mean this fellow all the newspapers are talking about.

FOSTER: Yes.

MAN: Of course I've heard of him.

FOSTER: Well, I'm his latest victim.

MAN: Victim! You mean …

FOSTER: I mean that he's cleared me out, Derek. Every penny. Every penny I ever made.

MAN: Good Heavens, old boy, that's terrible. How did it happen?

FOSTER: (*Quietly*) I don't know. At least not exactly.

MAN: But surely you …

FOSTER: About three weeks ago, I sold my business.

MAN: Oh, yes. I heard about that.

FOSTER: I sold it to Johnson and Wainwright. They gave me a cheque for twenty-eight thousand. That was on the Monday morning. At about two in the afternoon I paid it into the bank.

MAN: Well?

FOSTER: According to the Bank Manager I popped round again half an hour later and withdrew the entire amount. That was quite possible, by the way, I'd paid it into my credit account.

MAN: Well?

FOSTER: But, don't you see? I never returned to the bank. It was someone else. Someone who was clever enough to impersonate me so well that even the Bank Manager didn't notice the slightest difference.

MAN: (*Softly*) The Knave?

FOSTER: Obviously.

MAN: (*After a tiny pause*) How's Sheila taking all this?

FOSTER: She's been a brick, Derek. (*Suddenly*) I say, what are you doing?

MAN: (*After a tiny pause*) Nothing. (*After a second*) Now, take this cheque, Jim. It's for fifty-two quid. At present I can't afford any more, but the moment I ...

FOSTER: My dear fellow, if you think I could possibly ...

MAN: Oh lord, are you going to start that stuff! Now, take it, and don't be a mug!

FOSTER: Well – all right. But – but thanks awfully, Derek.

MAN: Forget it.

FADE IN of music.

Quick FADE DOWN.

MAN: Yes – I certainly felt sorry for Foster. He'd worked mighty hard all his life; and then suddenly to be cheated out of every penny was – well, to say the least of it, a jolly tough break. About a week after our meeting, he rang me up. "How about a spot of lunch?" he said. I said:

105

"Delighted." We met at The Savoy. By George, he looked different. Smart wasn't the word. He looked simply stunning. By some miraculous means or other he'd acquired a very delicate tan. "You're looking fit," I said. "Yes," he answered, "I've just had a month at Monte."

A slight pause.

MAN: Have you ever stared at anyone like an astonished mule? Well – that's precisely how I stared at Foster. Eventually – I said: "A month in Monte? What the Dickens do you mean, I met you in Regent Street about a week ago!" It was his turn to stare. "Impossible," he said, "I've been abroad for eight weeks." I didn't say anything. There was no need to. I guessed what had happened. And, of course, you've guessed too. I rang the bank up after lunch to see if my cheque had been cashed. The Manager was very amused. "You mean that one for fifty-two pounds?" he said. I said: "Yes, the cheque for fifty-two pounds." It had been cashed five days ago. Just as he was ringing off he said casually: "Did you put that five hundred on the Derby favourite?" "What five hundred?" I gasped. "The five hundred you drew out of the bank yourself – this morning." I'd never been near the bank that morning. I didn't say anything. There was no need to. I guessed what had happened. And, of course, you've guessed too!

THE END

THE ACE
Broadcast on BBC Radio
18th August 1936
in the revue *The Tune You Heard*

A new production of this sketch was included in *Five O'Clock Follies*, broadcast on 18 September 1937

Another new production was included in *Baker's Dozen*, broadcast on 16 November 1937

Another new production was included in *Mid-Week Matinée*, broadcast on 11 October 1939

Another new production was included in *Three Sketches by Francis Durbridge*, broadcast on 18 October 1940, featuring Bernadette Hodgson and Stuart Vinden

Another new production was included in the variety programme *Divertissement*, broadcast on 7 April 1941, featuring Marjorie Westbury and Alan Robinson

Another new production was included in the variety programme *Divertissement*, broadcast on 10 April 1943, featuring Patricia Hastings and Lewis Stringer

MAN: (*Rather a charming voice*) I'd always wanted the Fanshaw necklace, and I meant to get it. (*A slight pause*) The Fanshaw residence was one of those typical Mayfair mansions, grey and sombre, with several windows overlooking an untidy mews. I climbed into the library through one of those windows. It was a charming room, exquisitely furnished. The safe was concealed behind a bookcase, and in a very short while, I was staring at the Fanshaw necklace in the light of my torch. Suddenly I heard the click of a switch and the room was flooded with light. A girl stood in the doorway. It was obviously Tessa Fanshaw, although she seemed better looking than the pictures I had seen of her in the society papers. She carried a revolver. And the revolver was pointing at me. I smiled. I have a pleasant sort of smile and I intended her to notice it before she pulled the trigger of that revolver. She must have noticed it too, for instead of pulling the trigger, she said:

FADE IN music.

FADE quickly.

GIRL: Do you mind putting your hands up, please?

MAN: I beg your pardon?

GIRL: Your hands!

MAN: (*Casually*) Oh, I'm so sorry, I wasn't thinking.

A pause.

GIRL: You – you don't seem, very frightened.

MAN: Frightened? Of course I'm not frightened.

GIRL: You – you did intend to steal the pearls, didn't you?

MAN: Yes. Yes, of course. Are they yours?

GIRL: My mother's. I'll have them back, if you don't mind. (*After a tiny pause*) Thank you. (*Suddenly*) Oh, why did you come here? What made you choose this house?

MAN: I noticed your curtains. The pink curtains. Pink has always had a strange fascination for me. (*With a forced intonation*) I say, do you mind terribly if I put my hands down?

GIRL: (*After a tiny pause*) All right, but keep them out of your pockets.

MAN: Is that thing loaded?

GIRL: I don't know – yes – yes, of course it is.

A slight pause.

FADE IN of music.

FADE music.

MAN: You didn't mind my asking?

GIRL: Not at all. By the way, you don't happen to be the person all the papers are talking about, do you?

MAN: You mean 'The Ace?'

GIRL: Yes – 'The Ace.'

MAN: No, I'm afraid not. Sorry to disappoint you.

GIRL: Oh, I'm not disappointed. Somehow you don't look romantic.

MAN: Don't I? What a confounded nuisance! When I was dressing tonight, I said to myself: "John, you simply must look romantic ..."

GIRL: (*Puzzled*) Are you pulling my leg?

MAN: (*With mock seriousness*) Madam, I never mix pleasure with business.

GIRL: My word, you are an odd sort of individual.

MAN: Unique is the word, madam. Unique! Allow me, my card!

110

GIRL: (*Reading*) "John Conway. Gentleman of Leisure. Swindler. Cracksman. Professional Kleptomaniac. You have the best jewels. We want them." (*She starts laughing*) Now I know you're mad. Stark – staring mad!!!

MAN: On the contrary, madam, I'm particularly sane.

FADE IN of dance music.

FADE DOWN the music slowly.

MAN: I do wish you'd close that door! I'm finding it extremely difficult to be dignified with dance music punctuating my conversation.

The door closes.

GIRL: Is it necessary for you to be dignified?

MAN: Why, of course. There are only three types of burglars, madam. The dignified type, the melodramatic type and the bungling type. I was undecided at first whether to be dignified or melodramatic. As you see, I plumped for dignity.

GIRL: I suppose you'd call 'The Ace' a melodramatic type of burglar?

MAN: Why, naturally. Isn't it the height of melodrama always to leave the 'Ace of Diamonds' behind after committing a robbery? It's the sort of thing one reads about in twopenny thrillers. (*A shade melodramatic*) "And when morning came the jewels had vanished, but laid on the table with its face turned towards the doorway was – 'The Ace of Diamonds.'" (*He gives a little laugh*) I almost feel sorry I didn't go in for melodrama myself.

GIRL: In the papers they say that this fellow – 'The Ace' – always lets himself in by the front door. Do you think that's true?

111

MAN: (*With a laugh*) Well, from my extensive knowledge of front doors, I should say that was pretty well impossible!

GIRL: (*Quietly*) If I decided not to send for the police, would – would you give me a solemn promise never to do this again?

MAN: (*After a slight pause*) Yes. Yes, I would.

GIRL: Then I've decided quite definitely. I'm not going to hand you over to the police.

MAN: And I've decided quite definitely too. (*After a slight pause*) You're very sweet.

FADE IN music.

FADE music slowly.

MAN: The following morning I read about the robbery. It gave me rather a shock. Rather an unpleasant shock! The Fanshaw necklace had been stolen! Stolen by someone who had had the audacity to enter the house by the front door. (*Quietly*) A small playing card was found in the safe – the ace of diamonds. (*After a tiny pause*) I never knew 'The Ace' was a good looking girl of about twenty-seven – did you?

THE END

PAUL JONES
Broadcast on BBC Radio
12th February 1937
in *Variety in Miniature*
CAST:
Frankie . . .Barbara Helliwell
Paul . . . . .Hugh Morton

A new production of this sketch was included in *Mid-Week Matinée*, broadcast on 8 November 1939

Another new production, under the title *Cabaret*, was included in *Lunch Interval*, broadcast on 7 August 1941

Another new production, under the title *Cabaret*, was included in the revue *Cabaret*, broadcast on 13 June 1942

Another new production, under the title *Cabaret*, was included in *Revue for Two*, broadcast on 11 February 1943, featuring Marjorie Westbury and Dudley Rolph

OPEN TO:

A dance orchestra is playing.
SLOW FADE of the orchestra.

FRANKIE:	I should imagine you're the worst dancer in the world.
PAUL:	Not quite the worst. I have a brother.
FRANKIE:	I sincerely hope you haven't a sister to inflict your exhibitions upon.
PAUL:	I'm awfully sorry if I've hurt your feet at all.
FRANKIE:	You've ruined my shoes completely!
PAUL:	I'll buy you another pair.
FRANKIE:	I'm not in the habit of accepting presents from total strangers.
PAUL:	Oh! But I'm not a stranger. We've had three dances together.
FRANKIE:	I'm not likely to forget that fact.
PAUL:	After three dances I'm usually on very intimate terms with a girl.
FRANKIE:	After three of your dances, intimacy becomes a thing of the past.
PAUL:	I adore black shoes.
FRANKIE:	Mine were white originally!
PAUL:	(*Casually*) Black suits you better. Shall we sit down?
FRANKIE:	I was beginning to wonder why I ever left the dance floor.
PAUL:	You thought my company might be a little less revolting than my dancing.
FRANKIE:	It couldn't be worse!
PAUL:	As a matter of fact I'm a terrible dancer, but quite the best sitter out in the country.
FRANKIE:	They say practice makes perfect.
PAUL:	That's a fallacy. You see, Miss …?

FRANKIE:	Lawton.
PAUL:	(*Enthusiastically*) What a delightful name!
FRANKIE:	I'm so glad it meets with your approval.
PAUL:	As a matter of fact it doesn't. At least … not entirely. There ought to be something else. You know … a thingumbob.
FRANKIE:	You mean a Christian name?
PAUL:	Yes, that's it.
FRANKIE:	Oh! I have a Christian name.
PAUL:	I'm so pleased! (*A pause*) Do you ever use it?
FRANKIE:	My best friends use it quite often.
PAUL:	And what do your best friends call you, when they use it?
FRANKIE:	They call me 'Frankie.' Does that meet with your approval, Mr …?
PAUL:	Perfectly. And the name is Jones. Yes, Jones. My Grandfather was an original Jones, he kept a draper's shop in Aberavon.
FRANKIE:	My God! Jones! And the thingumbob?
PAUL:	The thingumbob?
FRANKIE:	The name your best friends call you by.
PAUL:	Well, as a matter of fact my best friends call me 'Stinker,' but I was christened 'Paul.'
FRANKIE:	Paul Jones!
PAUL:	Yes, Paul Jones. I had an uncle called 'Paul' and they named me 'Jones' after my Father.
FRANKIE:	I gathered that.

In the distant background the orchestra can be heard playing a rather sentimental waltz.

A slight pause.

FRANKIE:	Well?
PAUL:	For the last six months I've been living on my wits.
FRANKIE:	Are you forced to diet?

PAUL:	I'm serious. You see, I've been playing a not exactly honest game.
FRANKIE:	You mean you're a criminal?
PAUL:	(*Softly*) Yes. I came to this dance tonight for a definite purpose. To steal your necklace.
FRANKIE:	My necklace!

FRANKIE commences to laugh.

PAUL:	(*Amazed*) Why are you laughing?
FRANKIE:	The necklace happens to be paste – and not very good paste either!
PAUL:	Paste!
FRANKIE:	Yes. (*Amused*) We seem to have a great deal in common, Mr Jones. You see, I too came to this dance with a definite purpose in view.
PAUL:	You mean?
FRANKIE:	I stole your wallet ten minutes ago!

THE END

IN TRAINING
Broadcast on BBC Radio
6th September 1937
in *Follow On: a Revue in Miniature*

A new production of this sketch was included in *Mid-Week Matinée*, broadcast on 1 November 1939

Another new production was included in *Everything Stops for Tea*, broadcast on 1 September 1941

FADE IN of JACK laughing.

MICHAEL: What's the joke, Jack?

JACK: (*Still laughing*) I've just seen Dickie Rogers and Tommy Burke. Makes me laugh to even look at them!

MICHAEL: But why? What's funny about them? They look all right to me!

JACK: It's not their appearance, Michael. It's just that I always find myself thinking of a terribly funny experience that happened to the three of us last year.

MICHAEL: Oh ... what was it?

JACK: Well, Dickie, Tommy and I arrived at the station one night, about six o'clock. The train was late getting in, so we ... we ... popped round to the ... er ... local and had a little ... er ... light refreshment.

MICHAEL: Well?

JACK: When we returned to the station the platform was still empty, and a porter told us that the train was much later than they had expected. So naturally, Tommy, Dickie and I decided to ...

MICHAEL: (*Amused*) Return for more light refreshment?

JACK: Mm'm ... exactly.

MICHAEL: Well?

JACK: Well ... eventually we returned once again to the station. The platform was still empty! The train was still late! So naturally our first thought was for ...

MICHAEL: More light refreshment!

JACK: (*Laughing*) Exactly! For the fourth time we arrived at the station, and believe it or not ...

MICHAEL: (*Rather bored*) The train was still late.

JACK:	No jolly fear! It was almost steaming out of the station! The three of us raced down the platform – and Dickie and Tommy just managed to jump into the last compartment.
MICHAEL:	But … but, what happened to you?
JACK:	I was left on the platform! (*Very amused*) Simply howling with laughter! (*He chuckles*)
MICHAEL:	(*Puzzled*) You howled with laughter?
JACK:	Yes.
MICHAEL:	I thought you said they caught the train – and you didn't?
JACK:	(*Laughing*) That's just it! They were seeing me off!

THE END

THE CUSTOMER
IS ALWAYS RIGHT
Broadcast on BBC Radio
19th October 1939
in *Everything Stops for Tea*

A new production of this sketch was included in *Everything Stops for Tea*, broadcast on 8 May 1942

OPEN TO:

A door opens and closes.

MAN: Good morning, sir.

CUSTOMER: Good morning.

MAN: It's a very nice morning, sir.

CUSTOMER: That's entirely a matter of opinion.

MAN: Well – er – what can I get you, sir?

CUSTOMER: I should like a hat. A soft hat.

MAN: A soft hat? Certainly, sir. Try this for size.

CUSTOMER: M'm – much too large.

MAN: It seems to fit all right, sir.

CUSTOMER: Nevertheless, it's too large. I want a small soft hat.

MAN: A small soft hat … certainly, sir. Now how does this sort of thing appeal to you?

CUSTOMER: It doesn't.

MAN: Absolutely the latest style, sir.

CUSTOMER: I didn't come here to discuss styles or anything else. I want a hat. A soft hat. A small soft hat.

MAN: We couldn't interest you in a bowler, sir?

CUSTOMER: Definitely not.

MAN: Or possibly a topper, sir?

CUSTOMER: I should loathe and detest a topper.

MAN: I think I know what you want, sir. A soft hat?

CUSTOMER: Exactly.

MAN: A small soft hat?

CUSTOMER: Precisely.

MAN: Well, how's this, sir?

CUSTOMER: M'm – is this the smallest hat you've got in the shop?

MAN: Absolutely!

CUSTOMER: The softest?

MAN:	Positively.
CUSTOMER:	I'll take it.
MAN:	Yes – but it – er – won't suit you, sir!
CUSTOMER:	That doesn't matter.
MAN:	It won't – er – fit you, sir.
CUSTOMER:	That's quite unimportant.
MAN:	But … But … I don't understand.
CUSTOMER:	Young man … there's a war on … a war on …
MAN:	Yes, I know, but …
CUSTOMER:	Well … I didn't think there was going to be a war. D'you hear that? I didn't think there was going to be a war!
MAN:	But what the deuce has that got to do with your hat?
CUSTOMER:	My dear fellow, I don't think you quite understand! I've got to eat it!!!!

THE END

PARENTS
Broadcast on BBC Radio
19th October 1939
in *Everything Stops for Tea*

COMPERE: Ladies and gentlemen – for the benefit of the younger members of our audience we are going to demonstrate in our next sketch how parents have changed both in outlook, manner, and behaviour during the past century. Our first scene takes place in 1839.

MOTHER: Augustus, wake up! Wake up, Augustus!

FATHER: (*Sleepily*) Good Lord, what is it? What is it, mother?

MOTHER: (*Terribly distressed*) It's Jennifer – she's eloped!

FATHER: Eloped! Eloped! – did ye say? My God, Martha! Find me trousers, Martha. Find me trousers!!!

MOTHER: (*Weeping*) Oh Jennifer! Oh Jennifer!!

FATHER: Who is it? Who is the blackguard?

MOTHER: Jonathan Browne.

FATHER: (*Convulsed with fury*) What!! Jonathan Browne? My God, Martha! I'll call the police! I'll call the fire brigade! I'll call the mayor!

MOTHER: She – left this note.

FATHER: Read it! Read it!

MOTHER: (*Reading*) "Dearest Mother – I've eloped with Jonathan Browne – will write you from Brighton."

FATHER: Brighton! Brighton! D'you hear that, Martha? City of sin! City of sin!!!!

COMPERE: And now ladies and gentlemen for the same scene, only this time in 1939.

MOTHER: Arthur, wake up! Arthur, wake up!

FATHER: (*Sleepily*) What is it? What's the matter?

129

MOTHER: It's Jenny – she's eloped.

FATHER: (*Going back to sleep*) Oh.

MOTHER: I say, Arthur – I hope she's all right.

FATHER: Course she's all right. Pop off to bed, there's a good –

MOTHER: But she could be in danger!

FATHER: Nonsense! Who's the fellow?

MOTHER: Jonathan Browne.

FATHER: Good Lord! Fancy that! I knew his mother – er – rather well.

MOTHER: Jenny left this note.

FATHER: A note eh? Let's have a look. (*Agitated*) I say, that's a bit thick!

MOTHER: (*Alarmed*) What's the matter, dear?

FATHER: (*Angrily*) That's too much of a good thing!!

MOTHER: What is it, Arthur?

FATHER: (*Annoyed*) My God, Martha, if …

MOTHER: Arthur! What is it?

FATHER: She's left the "g" out of Brighton. Last week she missed an "L" out of Llandudno, and the week before she spelt Felixstowe with an "r". (*Furiously*) Something must be done about that girl, Martha. She's a lousy speller!

THE END

THE DAILY DODGE

A Family Affair

Broadcast on BBC Radio
4th April – 27th June 1939
Written by Durbridge and Archie Campbell,
included in the fortnightly
magazine programme *For You, Madam*

CAST:

Mrs Dodge . . . . Kathleen Harrison
Robert Clayton . . . . Edgar Norfolk
Lucy Clayton . . . . . Hilda Bruce Potter
Jane Clayton . . . . .Pamela Nell
Norman Clayton . . . . .Leonard Thorne

EPISODE ONE

FADE IN of a gong.

It is a small breakfast gong, while the gong is heard the voices of JANE and NORMAN CLAYTON can also be heard in the background, they are obviously quarrelling.

LUCY: (*Shouting – rather wearily*) Do hurry up, children! Your father's waiting …

NORMAN: (*Shouting from the background*) It's Jane, mother! She won't let me have the towel!

JANE: (*Also in the background*) Oh, do shut up, you little beast!

JANE and NORMAN continue to quarrel.

FADE voices.

We are now at the breakfast table with ROBERT and LUCY CLAYTON.

ROBERT: (*Looking at his watch*) Tt – Tt. Twenty minutes past eight. We're going to be late this morning, Lucy.

LUCY: (*Obviously rather depressed*) Well, I've told them at least half a dozen times, Robert – I can't do any more.

ROBERT: All right, my dear. All right! There's no need to get irritable about it!

LUCY: Tt. Tt. I do wish Jane would hurry.

JANE arrives. She is a very self-confident girl.

JANE: Good morning, mother! Good morning, daddy!

LUCY: You're terribly late, Jane. Your father's almost ready.

JANE: It doesn't matter, I only want a cup of tea. That little beast Norman kept me waiting hours for the bathroom.

ROBERT: Don't talk about your brother like that, Jane. It isn't nice!

JANE: Oh, all right.

135

LUCY: I think you'd better go on ahead without Norman
            this morning, Robert – otherwise you'll be late.

ROBERT: No. He'll have to do without his breakfast – it'll
            teach him to get up at a proper time of a
            morning. Instead of just laying in bed and … oh
            there you are, young man!

NORMAN is a rather cheeky fellow of about fifteen.

NORMAN: Hello! Oh, Lord, isn't there any coffee – I hate
            tea!

JANE: I can't understand why your Lordship doesn't
            have breakfast served in the bathroom.

NORMAN: Not so much of the wisecracking sister!

ROBERT: For goodness sake, don't talk in that awful slang
            – and if you want any breakfast be quick and get
            it, we're late already.

NORMAN: All right – all right. I don't want anything
            anyway. Gee, I don't know why we can't have
            coffee in the morning.

JANE: You can't expect mother to make coffee just for
            you. In any case, it's not good for you on an
            empty stomach.

NORMAN: Oh, pipe down, Jane!

LUCY: Norman, will you please do as your father tells
            you and stop using that awful language!

NORMAN: Well, she started it!

JANE: No, I didn't. All I said was that you couldn't
            expect mother to make coffee just because …

NORMAN: Oh, shut up! Gosh, Joe must be crazy to take a
            girl like you to the pictures.

JANE: We don't go to the pictures.

NORMAN: No, you sit in the front room all night and hold
            hands.

JANE: (*Indignantly*) That's a lie!!!!

NORMAN: No it isn't – I've seen you!!!

136

JANE: You little beast – spying!!!!

LUCY: Children, please! Please!!!!

ROBERT: (*Suddenly*) Sh! Listen! What's that?

Someone is knocking on the kitchen door.

LUCY: Goodness me, it's Mrs Dodge!

ROBERT: Mrs Dodge!

LUCY: We <u>are</u> late!

ROBERT: (*Briskly*) I'm off, mother. Come along, Norman. Get your coat, Jane.

LUCY: (*With a sigh of relief*) Goodbye, Robert.

ROBERT: Goodbye, dear. Don't expect I'll be late tonight.

JANE: Goodbye, mum!

NORMAN: Goodbye, mum!

JANE and NORMAN continue to chatter in excited voices.

FADE voices.

A door closes.

The sound of the breakfast paraphernalia being moved.

Another door opens.

LUCY: Good morning, Mrs Dodge.

MRS DODGE: Good morning, mum. I'm a bit early like this morning – got a lift 'ere in a lorry. Young Harry Turner picked me up just as I was getting on the tram. (*Laughing*) He's a caution that one, an' no mistake. (*Looking round the kitchen*) Now where's my apron? Oh, here we are! Blimey, it's a bit off colour, isn't it? We'd better pop it in the wash.

The lid of the boiler is heard.

MRS DODGE: How's the Master's cough, mum, any better?

LUCY: (*Obviously thinking of something else*) Yes, it's much better, thanks …

137

MRS DODGE:	Now we'll be wanting this petticoat, won't we? (*After a slight pause*) You're the one that's a bit off-colour if you ask me …
LUCY:	(*Quietly*) Oh, I'm all right …
MRS DODGE:	(*Shrewdly*) Nothing the matter, mam, I 'ope …
LUCY:	No, there's nothing the matter only … only … (*Suddenly*) Mrs Dodge … I've been thinking a great deal about things lately and … and …
MRS DODGE:	Blimey, I 'ope you're not going to give me the sack!
LUCY:	(*Laughing*) No. No, nothing like that … As a matter of fact, I rather hoped that you might be able to help me.
MRS DODGE:	Anything to oblige, mam, I'm sure.
LUCY:	You're a woman of experience, Mrs Dodge, and …
MRS DODGE:	Well, I've 'ad five youngsters, mam – but I don't know as how I shall call it experience exactly. The first was more in the nature of a surprise as you might say.
LUCY:	No, I mean you've had experience of life and of people. You see things in rather a different way.
MRS DODGE:	(*Quietly*) I've 'ad to, mum – when I was sixteen things was more or less "up to me" as you might say.
LUCY:	Yes. Yes, I know. (*Suddenly*) Mrs Dodge … I'm thinking of going away …
MRS DODGE:	(*Surprised and rather puzzled*) Going away …?
LUCY:	Yes.
MRS DODGE:	You mean on … on a sort of 'oliday, mam?

138

LUCY:	(*Quietly*) Yes, on a … sort of holiday …

A slight pause.

MRS DODGE:	Alone?
LUCY:	Yes, quite alone …
MRS DODGE:	Well, it's none of my business, mam – but you said I might be able to 'elp and if you wants my advice then …
LUCY:	(*Earnestly*) Oh, I do, Mrs Dodge! I do!!!!
MRS DODGE:	(*With warmth*) Then what is it, dearie? What's worrying you?

A slight pause.

LUCY:	Mrs Dodge, I'm tired … oh not physically … I'm just tired of (*Fervently*) I'm tired to death of getting up on a morning and cooking the breakfast … I'm tired of squabbling over the bathroom … of calling the children … of arguing with the milkman … of making the beds. I'm tired of the neighbours … of Robert … of the children … and even, just a little bit of you, Mrs Dodge!
MRS DODGE:	(*Quietly*) And so you're thinking of going away?
LUCY:	Yes. (*Suddenly*) Oh, I know it all sounds silly and unusual, but as far as I can see it's the …
MRS DODGE:	No, mam, it's not a bit silly – and 'eaven only knows it's not a bit irregular as you might say. Oh, there are millions of Mrs Clayton's in this 'ere world with just the same sort of 'ubbys, the same sort o' children, the same sort of neighbours, and, believe it or not, the same sort of "want" to get away from it all.

139

LUCY: But – but what am I going to do, Mrs Dodge? I can't go on like this day in and day out unless I –

MRS DODGE: You asked my advice, mam ... but if I gives it will you take it now ...?

LUCY: Of course ... of course, Mrs Dodge!

MRS DODGE: And no 'ard feelings?

LUCY: No. No, of course not.

MRS DODGE: (*Decisively*) Then go upstairs, mam, an' pack your bag!

LUCY: (*Surprised and now just a shade frightened at the thought*) Pack ... Pack my bag ...

MRS DODGE: Yes, mam – an' then scribble a note to your 'ubby telling 'im exactly 'ow you feel.

LUCY: Oh, but ... but I couldn't do that. I should have to see him first and explain or he'd ...

MRS DODGE: (*With a touch of authority*) Now, mam, this is my advice, if you don't want to take it then ...

LUCY: No. No, please go on, Mrs Dodge.

MRS DODGE: Well, go upstairs, mam. Pack your bag. Scribble your note to the old man. Bring your bag downstairs – slip on your best 'of everything', and pop round to the butchers.

LUCY: (*Surprised*) The butchers ...?

MRS DODGE: That's right, mam. Order the juiciest bit o' steak in the place – and tell 'em to send it up quick. Then if you feel inclined drop in at that café in the High Street for a nice cup of coffee. As soon as you've had that come back 'ome, unpack your bag, tear up the note – and cook the fam'ly the biggest steak and kidney pud they've ever blinking well seen. And if the sight of their eyes popping out of their 'eads don't cure you … then me name's not Mrs Dodge … Now with your permission, mum, I'll get on with me washing. Now where did I put those darned soapflakes!

END OF EPISODE ONE

EPISODE TWO

OPEN TO:

MRS DODGE is very busy removing the teatime paraphernalia from the table.

ROBERT: Where's Mrs Clayton?

MRS DODGE: She's getting herself titivated up a bit. That's why I'm clearing the tea things.

Suddenly MRS DODGE drops the tray she is carrying ... there is a terrific smash of crockery.

MRS DODGE: (*Quiet unconcerned*) Tt ... Tt ... Butter fingers!

ROBERT: (*Irritated*) I thought you left at half past four, Mrs Dodge?

MRS DODGE: I does as a general rule, but the missis seemed in such a flurry I offered to give her a 'elping 'and. All going to the pictures, <u>aren't</u> you?

ROBERT: (*Obviously not pleased at the thought*) Mm – so I believe.

MRS DODGE: Coo – you sound happy about it, I must say!

The door opens.

JANE: (*Pleasantly, and in a great hurry*) I'm going now, father! Goodnight, Mrs Dodge!

ROBERT: (*Suddenly*) I say, just a minute ... just a minute. Where are you off to?

JANE: (*Impatiently*) The Palais de Danse ... I promised to meet Tom at seven ... if I don't hurry I'll be late.

ROBERT: Then you can be late for a change!

MRS DODGE: Keep him dangling, dearie. Does 'em all the world o' good.

ROBERT: That's all right, Mrs Dodge!

MRS DODGE: No offence – I'm sure!

JANE: What is it, father? I'm in a hurry!

145

ROBERT: Your mother told me that we were <u>all</u> going to the pictures?

JANE: Yes, I know … but I can't go. I promised Tom ages ago that I'd go to the Palais with him and if I started to back out now he'd only think that I …

ROBERT: All right! All right!!! But I don't know why on earth your mother takes the trouble to arrange these outings. You've always got something else on, Norman is always fiddling with his wireless, and I've always got a Lodge meeting I'd rather go to.

JANE: (*Amused*) Oh, so that's why you're so grumpy! Poor Daddy! Why don't you tell Mother you'd rather go to the meeting?

ROBERT: (*Disappointed*) No use! You know what your mother's like when she's got her mind set on something. You'd better slip out, Jane, while the going's good!

JANE: (*Laughing*) Righto! Goodnight, darling. Tell Mother I'm sorry. Goodnight, Mrs Dodge!

The door closes.

MRS DODGE: No flies on that one an' no mistake! I bet poor old Tom 'as his work cut out! (*After a slight pause*) Where do these cups go?

ROBERT: (*Obviously thinking of something else*) Mm – what's that?

MRS DODGE: Cups … cups … where do I put 'em?

ROBERT: Oh, on the sideboard for the time being … Mrs Clayton'll put them away …

MRS DODGE: Blimey, you're miles away, thinking of that Lodge meeting, I suppose?

ROBERT: Yes. Yes, I was as a matter of fact.

MRS DODGE: Why don't you tell the missis straight – you don't want to go to the pictures? Come to think of it she isn't so stuck on 'em herself.

ROBERT: Oh, well, she seems to have made her mind up, and I don't want to cause a fuss.

MRS DODGE: Supposing she changed 'er mind – about going to the pictures, I mean?

ROBERT: Oh, that would be fine. She wouldn't mind my going to the meeting at all then; providing <u>she</u> changed her mind. But it's no use my trying to persuade her because … oh, well, you know what women are!

MRS DODGE: I do. Don't think much of 'em myself! Can't trust 'em. You've been lucky an' got a good 'un …

ROBERT: (*Faintly amused*) How right you are, Mrs Dodge! (*With a sigh*) Still, I wish she didn't want to go to the films tonight!

The door opens.

LUCY: Oh, thank you, Mrs Dodge! It is good of you to stay behind. Get your shoes on, Norman!

NORMAN: Good Lord, Dad hasn't changed his suit yet …

ROBERT: No, and I'm not going to change it either!

LUCY: I do think you might have changed your suit, dear. There's always a lot of people we know there on a Saturday.

ROBERT: If the suit's good enough for the office, it's good enough for the pictures.

LUCY: Very well, dear. Here's your money, Mrs Dodge.

MRS DODGE: Thank you, mam. All goin' to the pictures, eh?

NORMAN:	All except Jane. She's out with Tom Warner ... Public Twerp Number 1!
LUCY:	(*Annoyed*) Norman, please! Mind what you're saying!
NORMAN:	Well, he is a ...
ROBERT:	(*Suddenly*) You heard what your mother said ... Now just you mind that tongue of yours, young man, or you'll be getting yourself into serious trouble!
NORMAN:	Yes, father!
LUCY:	Come along, Robert, we must hurry.
ROBERT:	(*Resigned*) Oh, very well, dear.
MRS DODGE:	Goodnight, mam. I 'ope you enjoy the film – it's ever so good ...
LUCY:	(*Pleased*) Oh, splendid! What's it called?
MRS DODGE:	Well, I don't rightly remember, but me an' the old man went last night. It was a rare treat. Ooh, but it did upset him. He went as white as a sheet ...
LUCY:	Why, what was the matter? Wasn't he well or something?
MRS DODGE:	Oh, yes, mam ... never felt better. It was the picture.
LUCY:	I thought you said it was good, Mrs Dodge?
MRS DODGE:	(*Enthusiastically*) Ooh, it is good. Ever so good. Fair gives you the creeps though ... Especially when the body comes to life ...
NORMAN:	Whose body?
MRS DODGE:	'Im that 'ad his throat sliced ...
NORMAN:	Coo!
MRS DODGE:	Yes, but I mustn't spoil it for you. It's ever such a surprise when you see the blood dripping. (*Abruptly changing the subject*) Now, where did I put that apron? Can't

	understand it, I always put me apron down an' then …
ROBERT:	(*Anxiously*) No, go on, Mrs Dodge … what sort of picture is it?
MRS DODGE:	I've told you! It's ever so good. Ooh, but that woman is wicked!!!
LUCY:	(*Slightly perturbed*) What … do … you mean 'wicked'?
MRS DODGE:	The things she gets up to! Well, honest … I didn't know what was going to 'appen next. I said to my old man, I'm a married woman myself but lord love a duck, them pictures can teach you a thing or two!!!
NORMAN:	(*Anxiously*) I say, come on, mum, or we won't get in before the show starts!
LUCY:	(*Perplexed*) I'm not at all sure that this is the sort of thing you ought to see, Norman. What do you think, Robert?
ROBERT:	Well … er … I … I leave it to you, dear.
MRS DODGE:	Oh, you must see it! My old man's going again in spite of turning queer. He says he wants to see the part where they push that poor old woman over the cliff. Cruelty! That's what I call it.
LUCY:	You know, Robert, I really don't think it sounds quite the sort of film Norman ought to see. He's got such an imagination. Now run along upstairs, Norman, and play your wireless set while I talk to your father.
NORMAN:	(*Bewildered*) What – what do you mean?
LUCY:	I don't think we'll go to the pictures tonight, darling! I've got rather a headache and perhaps the films would only …

NORMAN:	Well, blow me down! Of all the dirty tricks! I've washed my face and brushed my hair, and now we aren't even going out!
ROBERT:	Norman, didn't you hear your mother say she had a headache? Now run along upstairs and do as you're told.
NORMAN:	Oh, all right. Crikey!!!

The door closes.

ROBERT:	Really, there are times when that boy wants a jolly good whacking, mother! His manners are appalling!
LUCY:	Oh, he's disappointed because we're not going out, that's all.
MRS DODGE:	I'll take these dishes into the kitchen, ma'am.
LUCY:	Yes, very well, Mrs Dodge.

The door closes.

LUCY:	(*Whispering*) Robert, that film sounded dreadful, didn't it?
ROBERT:	Well, I must say, dear, it didn't sound exactly the sort of entertainment for Norman.
LUCY:	If it wasn't so late we could all go into Town ... but it's after seven now ...
ROBERT:	Yes.
LUCY:	Oh, well, I suppose I'd better get on with my sewing. I do hope Jane won't be disappointed.
ROBERT:	Oh no, I don't suppose she will be.

The door opens.

MRS DODGE:	Excuse me ... I meant to tell you, sir ... A Mr Jackson called round early this afternoon ... wanted to know if you was going to the Lodge meeting tonight.

150

ROBERT:	Oh, er – I see. Thank you, Mrs Dodge.
LUCY:	Lodge meeting ... tonight? I didn't know that, Robert. How nice for you. Don't you want to go?
ROBERT:	Oh well, I – er – don't mind if I do but ...
LUCY:	Well, there's no reason why you shouldn't go now since we're not going out to the pictures. That is, of course, if you want to ...
ROBERT:	Oh, very well, I might as well pop round for half an hour or so, I suppose.
LUCY:	I'll get your scarf, Robert, I've got to go upstairs for my sewing things.
ROBERT:	Thank you, mother.

A pause.
The door opens.

MRS DODGE:	Well, what happened?
ROBERT:	(*Puzzled*) What happened?
MRS DODGE:	Aren't you going to the Lodge meeting?
ROBERT:	Yes, I am, but ... (*Suddenly*) Good Lord ... (*Delighted*) I say, I've only just realised what's happened ... Then all that talk about the film was only to get ... I say, thanks a lot, Mrs Dodge ... Thanks a lot ...
MRS DODGE:	Oh, that's all right ... only too 'appy to be of service, I'm sure. But I 'ope to goodness the missis don't find out what's on at the blinkin' pictures.
ROBERT:	Why not?
MRS DODGE:	Crikey! The fat would be in the fire good an' proper. It's Snow White an' the blinkin' Dwarfs ...!!!

END OF EPISODE TWO

EPISODE THREE

FADE IN the sound of a vacuum cleaner together with the sound of MRS DODGE singing. It is difficult to distinguish between the noises.

The door opens.

NORMAN: What are you doing, Mrs Dodge?

MRS DODGE: What do you think I'm doing, dearie? Cleaning me teeth?

NORMAN: Mother won't like you using the vacuum on a Sunday.

MRS DODGE: There wouldn't be any need if you'd only eat your meals properly, 'stead of dropping egg all over the carpet.

NORMAN: It wasn't my fault! You can't expect a fellow to eat properly when his sister's pushing him all over the place.

MRS DODGE: If you was my kids I'd box your ears. Always squabbling at meals! I've never seen the likes of you.

NORMAN: (*Politely*) Are you Irish, Mrs Dodge?

MRS DODGE: Irish? Blimey, no, I'm a cockney.

NORMAN: Then don't say 'the likes of you' – with a cockney accent it sounds ludicrous.

MRS DODGE: Ludi-what?

NORMAN: Ludicrous.

MRS DODGE: (*Stopping the vacuum*) Listen to me, youngster, any more funny business from you and Bob's your Uncle!

NORMAN: (*Pleasantly*) O.K. Toots!

MRS DODGE: (*Staggered*) O.K. … Blimey!

The door opens.

ROBERT: Hello, Mrs Dodge – you seem pretty industrious for a Sunday.

MRS DODGE: Oh, I'm just doing a bit of tidying up, sir.

ROBERT:	Come along, Norman, or we shall be late for Church.
NORMAN:	There's no hurry, father, Jane isn't down yet.
ROBERT:	Your sister isn't coming to Church this morning, she's not feeling too well.
NORMAN:	(*Irritated*) Oh, well – all right!
ROBERT:	Good morning, Mrs Dodge!
MRS DODGE:	Good morning, sir.
NORMAN:	Goodbye, Mrs Dodge, keep on with the good work!
MRS DODGE:	Now youngster, don't be ludicri ... ludicru ... er ... ludicru-er- ... Scram!

The door shuts.

The vacuum continues.

The door opens.

It is MRS CLAYTON.

LUCY:	(*Surprised*) Whatever are you doing, Mrs Dodge?
MRS DODGE:	Don't worry, mum, I 'aven't started the spring cleaning. It's young Master Norman – he seems to 'ave been trying to make an egg sandwich out of the carpet!
LUCY:	Oh dear, these children are a problem! There's Jane moping about upstairs as if the end of the world had come, and there's Norman always going out of his way to use big words he doesn't even know the meaning of!
MRS DODGE:	I've had my basin full of that, this morning, mum. What's the matter with Miss Jane?
LUCY:	I don't know what it is, I'm sure, Mrs Dodge. I can't really get any sense out of her.

MRS DODGE: I expect she's had some sort of a tiff with Tom – you know what these young people are – always bleeding at the 'eart as you might say.

LUCY: Actually, Jane intended going away with Tom and his sister for Whitsun, but now Betty can't manage it for some reason or other. Naturally the trip has had to be cancelled. I rather think that's why Jane is so disagreeable.

MRS DODGE: Young people don't seem to be able to stand the disappointments nowadays, do they, mum?

LUCY: Jane has been trying to persuade us to let her go on her own – with Tom I mean. But I don't really think that's right, do you, Mrs Dodge? Not that we've anything against Tom, he's really an awfully nice fellow – but naturally one has got to be so very careful.

MRS DODGE: Does she want to go with him?

LUCY: Yes, I'm rather afraid she does, but her father won't hear of it. Oh, well – I must be off, Mrs Dodge, or I shall be late for Church. Don't bother about the carpet – we can brush that off tomorrow sometime.

MRS DODGE: If it's all the same to you, mum, I'll finish it off proper.

The door closes.
The vacuum continues then suddenly stops.

JANE: Have the others gone, Mrs Dodge?

MRS DODGE: Yes, they've just left, dearie. Blimey, you look a little ray of sunshine I must say!

JANE:	Oh, I'm all right. What's it like out, Mrs Dodge?
MRS DODGE:	Not bad – wireless was wrong again as usual. I reckon it'll turn out nice for Whitsun.
JANE:	(*Petulantly*) I don't care if it rains the whole of Whitsun, so there!
MRS DODGE:	Oh, don't say that, dearie. Think of the hikers. If it rains they'll blinkin' well 'ave to hike.
JANE:	I'm afraid my plans have gone completely cock-eyed.
MRS DODGE:	Yes, so I 'eard.
JANE:	I was going away with Tom and his sister Betty, but now Betty can't manage it so we've had to cancel the trip. It's father's fault really, he's so dreadfully old-fashioned.
MRS DODGE:	What's the old man got to do with it?
JANE:	Well, I don't see why I shouldn't go with Tom – do you, Mrs Dodge?
MRS DODGE:	You mean just the two of you?
JANE:	Why, yes, of course! Good heavens, don't say you're shocked, Mrs Dodge. This is 1939, you know, not the middle-ages!
MRS DODGE:	Judging from what the newspapers tell us, duckie, there ain't a 'ell of a lot of difference.
JANE:	I wish Daddy would see sense. It's so silly doing this heavy father stuff with Tom. We're not a couple of kids.
MRS DODGE:	What does Tom think about it?
JANE:	He thinks the same as I do, of course. It's just a lot of nonsense!

158

MRS DODGE:	Where did you reckon on going?
JANE:	Well, we did reckon on Brighton.
MRS DODGE:	Brighton! You might 'ave picked on somewhere a little more reserved, dearie.
JANE:	I don't really mind where we go so long as we get away. The thought of having to spend Whitsun with the family nearly drives me frantic!
MRS DODGE:	Yes, you look as if you need a bit of a change, I must admit. Would your old man object to the 'oliday if Tom's sister could go?
JANE:	Good heavens no! As long as we have a chaperone he doesn't care twopence! I don't know why he doesn't dress me up in crinolines and have done with it.
MRS DODGE:	I suppose the family aren't going away?
JANE:	No. They'll just laze about as usual. Except of course Norman and he'll spend the entire holiday pestering Daddy, and everybody else, because he hasn't got a bike. I wish to goodness somebody would buy him a bike – it might keep him quiet for a month or two.
MRS DODGE:	Isn't there anyone else you could ask to go with you, dearie, besides Tom's sister?
JANE:	No one we'd care to have with us, Mrs Dodge. That's one thing I'll say for Betty, she does keep to herself.
MRS DODGE:	(*Thoughtfully*) I've just been thinking, duckie. Why don't you take Norman?
JANE:	(*Astounded*) Norman? You mean … <u>our</u> … Norman?
MRS DODGE:	That's the Norman I mean, dearie.

JANE:	Why, why he'd be impossible. He'd follow us about like a trailer. He'd want to go everywhere with us ... Why, Good Lord, I can just imagine what Tom would say if I suggested it.
MRS DODGE:	Do you think your old man would approve?
JANE:	Approve? Daddy would jump at it! He'd even pay his expenses. The very thought of getting rid of Norman for a few days would make a new man out of him.
MRS DODGE:	Then why don't you take him?
JANE:	I've told you why! He'd be impossible. You've no idea what he's like on holiday, Mrs Dodge! We shouldn't have a minute to ourselves. It'd be just a sheer waste of time going away ...
MRS DODGE:	(*Quietly*) I don't think so, dearie, not if you handled him properly!
JANE:	(*After a slight pause*) What do you mean?
MRS DODGE:	I don't see why you couldn't take Norman and then let him more or less go off on his own.
JANE:	But he wouldn't go off on his own, Mrs Dodge!!!!
MRS DODGE:	(*Softly*) He might.
JANE:	You don't know Norman!!!!
MRS DODGE:	And you don't know Mrs Dodge!
JANE:	(*Puzzled*) What do you mean ...?
MRS DODGE:	(*Slowly*) Supposing you hired a bike for him, dearie, just ... for ... a ... couple ... of ... days ...
JANE:	(*Amazed*) Hired a bike for him ... Hired a ... (*Suddenly very happy*) Mrs Dodge! Mrs Dodge, you're a genius!!!!

MRS DODGE: I wish you'd tell my old man.
They both roar with laughter.

END OF EPISODE THREE

EPISODE FOUR

FADE UP of NORMAN playing the piano – needless to say, he is playing extremely badly.

JANE: Oh, there you are, Norman! I've been looking all over the house for you!

NORMAN: Why?

JANE: I suppose you know what day it is tomorrow?

NORMAN: Course I know – it's Wednesday.

JANE: I don't mean that, stupid!

The piano stops.

NORMAN: (*Quietly*) You mean it's … Mother's birthday?

JANE: Yes, and I do think it's mean of you, Norman, not going half with me over those gloves. They cost eight and six, and I really think …

NORMAN: But, I've told you, Jane, I can't afford it. I owe Mrs Dodge two bob, and I've promised to …

JANE: (*Bewildered*) But – But aren't you going to buy Mother anything?

NORMAN: (*Evasively*) I … I don't know. I haven't thought about it.

JANE: Then it's about time you did think about it! Really, Norman, I do think it's a bit thick. I told Father you wouldn't go half with me over the gloves, and he was furious.

NORMAN: (*Worried and annoyed*) Crikey, Jane, what did you want to tell father for? He's ratty enough with me for messing up the wireless, without you piling on the agony.

The door opens.

ROBERT: Has either of you seen your mother?

JANE: She's upstairs, I think, father – with Mrs Dodge.

ROBERT: Oh, I see. No, don't go, Norman … I want to have a talk with you. Tell mother I'd like to see her later, Jane.

165

JANE:	All right, Father.

The door closes.

ROBERT:	(*Clearing his throat*) Mm … Jane tells me that you won't go half with her over a birthday present for your mother …
NORMAN:	Well, you see, father … for several weeks now I've been saving up because …
ROBERT:	Because you want to buy a bicycle … I know. Well, it seems to me that you might forget that for a little while and give your mother some consideration instead.
NORMAN:	But, father, what I was going to say was simple …
ROBERT:	Now, listen, Norman. If you don't mind, I'll do the talking for a change. I've been meaning to have a chat with you for some time. For some unknown reason you seem to be developing not merely an extremely selfish side to your nature, but also …
NORMAN:	(*Rather hurt*) But, Father …
ROBERT:	As I was saying – you also seem to be going out of your way to make yourself look as … as … unpresentable as possible. Just look at yourself. No, I'm not joking, Norman! Have a good look at yourself! Your hair's untidy, your face is smudgy, and your tie is all over the place.
NORMAN:	Well, you can't expect me to look like Robert Taylor! (*Still cheeky, but obviously upset by his father's attitude*) You'll … you'll be wanting me to manicure my fingernails next!
ROBERT:	I don't know about fingernails, young man, but, unless you very quickly mend your

ways, you'll find yourself on intimate terms with a hairbrush! Do I make myself clear?

NORMAN: (*Almost weeping*) Y-yes, father.

ROBERT: Well ... we ... we won't say any more for the present. But just make some attempt to mend your ways, and – remember – selfishness doesn't pay in the long run.

NORMAN: But, dad, I don't think you understand. I wasn't forgetting about mother's birthday ... honestly, I ...

ROBERT: That's all for the present, Norman. Just think over what I've been saying.

The door closes.

NORMAN: (*Bitterly*) Yes ... Yes, father. (*To himself*) It ... it isn't fair ... It isn't fair ... (*He is more upset than ever now that ROBERT has departed*) It isn't as if I blinkin' well meant to ... to ... Oh, crikey!!!

The door opens.

MRS DODGE enters.

MRS DODGE: Blimey, you've been 'aving a basin full of 'appiness, by the look of yer. What's up, duckie?

NORMAN: It's Father. He's been on at me about Mother's birthday.

MRS DODGE: Oh, yes ... I 'eard about that. Miss Jane wanted you to go 'alf with her over a pair of gloves or something.

NORMAN: Yes, that's right. But I couldn't, Mrs Dodge, because you see, I've spent all my money on something else. Something for mother, I mean.

MRS DODGE: (*Excited*) You 'ave! What is it?

NORMAN: It's a vase, Mrs Dodge. An absolute corker! You know mother says she can never find one big enough. Well, I saw this one in that new auction room opposite the post office. Cost over a quid … I've been saving up for weeks!

MRS DODGE: (*Surprised*) But … but … doesn't Jane know about this, or your dad?

NORMAN: Nobody knows. I've been keeping it a dead secret.

The door opens.

JANE: (*Dumping a parcel on the table*) Oh, Norman, this parcel's just arrived. It's for you, apparently.

NORMAN: Oh … er … thanks!

The door closes.

MRS DODGE: Would this be the … er … thingymebob?

NORMAN: Yes … I expect so.

MRS DODGE: Let's 'ave a squint at it!

NORMAN: O.K. But keep 'cave'.

The parcel is unwrapped.

MRS DODGE: Blimey!

NORMAN: (*Anxiously*) Don't you like it?

MRS DODGE: (*Doubtfully*) Oh, yes, I like it all right. Ever so gaudy though, ain't it?

NORMAN: I don't believe you <u>do</u> like it, Mrs Dodge.

MRS DODGE: Oh, yes, I do. But it proper takes your breath away, doesn't it?

NORMAN: I hope it'll surprise mum.

MRS DODGE: Surprise her? It'll knock 'er off 'er pedestal, good an' proper. And won't yer dad be surprised?

NORMAN: Yes, I do hope Father likes it, because … (*Suddenly*) … Careful, Mrs Dodge!

MRS DODGE: Don't worry, sonny. I shan't drop it. Blimey, the more yer looks at it, the more it dazzles yer. Talk about the stars and stripes!

NORMAN: The man in the shop said it could never be duplicated, no matter how hard you tried.

MRS DODGE: He did, did he? Well, that's something to be thankful for.

NORMAN: I'll take it now, Mrs Dodge.

A slight pause.

NORMAN: Now we must be careful how we pack it up, because …

MRS DODGE: (*Suddenly*) Look out!!!!

The vase falls with a crash.

MRS DODGE: Whoops, dearie, that's done it! I told you to look out.

NORMAN: Oh, look at the vase! (*Very upset*) Just look at the vase, Mrs Dodge!

MRS DODGE: I'm looking at it! Crikey! 'Ell of a mess, ain't it? You must have tripped over the lid.

NORMAN: Oh, golly! What am I going to do? … What on earth am I going to do?

MRS DODGE: (*In a fluster*) Now, keep calm – keep calm, duckie. Don't get yerself all flustered.

NORMAN: (*Nearly crying*) But, you don't understand. Now they'll all be convinced that I forgot Mother's birthday and Dad will …

MRS DODGE: No, they won't. Not if you tell 'em about it and show 'em the bits and pieces.

NORMAN: Yes, and I can just imagine what Father would say – "Careless, again, as usual".

MRS DODGE: (*Suddenly*) I've got it! Why don't you parcel it up and then when it arrives you can pretend it's been and got itself knocked about on the way.

NORMAN: That's an idea, Mrs Dodge. (*Thoughtfully*)
            Yes, that's an idea ...

FADE SCENE.

FADE IN all members of the family singing She's A Jolly Good Fellow.

LUCY: Well, thanks for all the lovely presents.
            You've been far too kind and generous.
            Now come along and finish your breakfast,
            or you'll all be late.

JANE: I think Norman might have bought you
            something ...

LUCY: Please, Jane, you mustn't say things like
            that.

The door opens.

MRS DODGE enters.

MRS DODGE: Another parcel, mum. Just arrived ... Looks
            as if it's been knocked about a bit in the
            post, I must say.

LUCY: Thanks, Mrs Dodge. (*Suddenly*) No, Jane,
            leave it alone. I'll undo it.

The parcel is unwrapped.

LUCY: What a lot of tissue paper. There's a card,
            too. (*Reading*) "To Mother – wishing her
            many happy returns of the day – from
            Norman". Oh, Norman, how sweet of you!
            Now, I wonder what it can be!

ROBERT: Whatever it is, it's all in pieces.

LUCY: Oh, so it is – and such a lovely vase!

JANE: Oh, Norman, I <u>am</u> sorry! What beastly luck!

MRS DODGE: Shame, I call it – what them postmen get up
            to!

LUCY: Never mind, Norman, darling. It shows how
            thoughtful you were after all.

ROBERT:	Very good of you, Norman! Very good of you, indeed.
NORMAN:	Thank you, father. Well, I … er … think I'll run along and get my cap. Shan't be long …

The door shuts.

ROBERT:	That was really very decent of Norman, I must say. I shall have to revise my opinion of that young man. He's not so bad … Wait a minute, though … Something's just struck me …
LUCY:	What do you mean, Robert?
ROBERT:	The way this vase is wrapped up … You did say the postman brought it, didn't you, Mrs Dodge?
MRS DODGE:	Er – yes, sir.
ROBERT:	You're quite sure, Mrs Dodge?
MRS DODGE:	As sure as my …
ROBERT:	Well, just take another look here, will you? He must have been a very careful postman.
MRS DODGE:	Blimey! What'll that boy be up to next? He's been and wrapped up every piece … SEPARATE!!!

END OF EPISODE FOUR

EPISODE FIVE

ROBERT: I say these thingemebobs are pretty good for the time of the year, aren't they?

LUCY: Which thingemebobs, darling?

ROBERT: (*Laughing*) I mean these ramblers, Lucy.

LUCY: (*Also laughing*) Yes, but do leave them alone, Robert, remember what Mr Middleton said about …

ROBERT: (*Pleasantly*) I may not be Mr Middleton, my dear, but I do know how to treat a rambler. Now just stop nagging!

LUCY: (*With a pleasant sigh*) All right, Robert. All right.

ROBERT: (*After a pause*) Nice in the garden tonight, eh?

LUCY: Oh, it's so lovely, Robert. And <u>so</u> peaceful.

ROBERT: (*Obviously giving something his attention*) Yes … nice to have the kids back again, too … Seem to have enjoyed themselves all right.

LUCY: (*With a laugh*) They've had a marvellous time from all accounts. According to Jane poor old Norman seems to have spent his entire weekend in the fair ground.

ROBERT: (*Amused*) I wonder what he thinks he's going to do with all those coconuts?

LUCY: Well, he certainly isn't going to eat them, I'll see to that! (*Suddenly*) I say, Robert!

ROBERT: What is it, dear?

LUCY: Isn't that the children …?

FADE IN very slowly the sound of angry voices.

ROBERT: (*Quietly*) By jingo … Listen to 'em …

FADE IN JANE and NORMAN. They are in the middle of a really heated argument.

JANE: I wish you'd mind your own business, Norman! It isn't anything to do with you in any case.

NORMAN: Oh, yes, it is something to do with me. I won't have you going about with someone you hardly know. It isn't fair to Tom.

JANE: Oh, you're very friendly towards Tom all of a sudden! I shall go about with just whoever I want to go about with, and I shan't ask your permission, my lord.

NORMAN: Oh, no, you won't!

JANE: (*Furious*) I like your confounded impudence, Norman, I must say! Trying to tell me what to do and who to go out with …

NORMAN: (*Rather concerned*) Listen, sis, I'm not trying to be funny about this business. Honestly, I'm not. But, well …

JANE: Well, what?

NORMAN: Well … Larry isn't the sort of fellow you ought to knock about with. He's smart I suppose an' all the rest of it but …

JANE: But, my dear Norman, I'm not knocking about with him. I'm only going for a ride in his car.

NORMAN: Yes, well, I don't think you ought to!

JANE: And why not …?

NORMAN: Well, because … because you hardly know anything at all about him … and … because it's not fair to Tom … an' … an' … oh, because he's a twerp!

JANE: You're just like a baby, Norman. Just because I'm going for a ride with Larry it doesn't mean to say …

NORMAN: You're not going for a ride with him – not if I can stop it!

JANE: (*Angrily*) All right, Mr Clever, we'll see about that!

The door closes with a bang.

The piano starts.

NORMAN is practising but he is not really interested in what he is doing.

MRS DODGE enters.

MRS DODGE: What's that you're playing – Jeepers Creepers?

NORMAN: No, it's … These Foolish Things.

MRS DODGE: It's a pity you can't use the black notes, duckie, it makes such a difference.

NORMAN: (*He stops playing. To himself*) I can't understand Jane, she must be crazy.

MRS DODGE: Why, what's the matter with 'er?

NORMAN: Oh, she's going out for a ride with a chap we met at Brighton over the weekend. The little tyke!

MRS DODGE: But what about this other bloke … Tom …?

NORMAN: Oh, she's still pally with Tom, but this other chap happened to have a car and …

MRS DODGE: That's enough, dearie! I've been to the pictures!

NORMAN: I wouldn't mind, but … he's such a frightful little beast. (*Worried*) Oh dear, I do wish Jane would see some sense!

MRS DODGE: Blimey, you look pretty miserable about it, I must say. Anybody'd think she was walking out with the Dead-End kids!!!!

NORMAN: (*Seriously*) Mrs Dodge … do help me … He's not at all the right sort of person for Jane to go out with.

MRS DODGE: (*Thoughtfully*) You say he's coming 'ere in 'is car?

NORMAN: Yes … Oh, dear … I don't know what to do I'm sure.

FADE IN the sound of a car.

MRS DODGE: Listen …
NORMAN: Mrs Dodge, this … this is …
MRS DODGE: (*Quickly*) Wait 'ere, dearie. I shan't be a
               minute.
NORMAN: (*Excitedly*) Where are you going?
MRS DODGE: (*Already across the room*) I shan't be a
               minute!

The door opens.

JANE pops her head round the door.

JANE: When the bell rings tell Mrs Dodge to
               answer the door.
NORMAN: Oh, all right.
JANE: I'll be in the garden if I'm wanted.

The door closes.

After a tiny pause MRS DODGE returns.

MRS DODGE: 'Ere we are … This'll do the trick.
NORMAN: But – but what is it?
MRS DODGE: A chisel, dearie. You only 'ave to dig it in
               'is tyres an' phew! Bob's your uncle!
NORMAN: (*Excited*) But, Mrs Dodge!
MRS DODGE: Now be careful, don't let the old man catch
               you! If I 'ear anybody coming I'll sing.
               Even if <u>you</u> don't 'ear me, it'll scare 'em
               away!
NORMAN: (*Excited*) Righto, Mrs Dodge!

A door opens.

We are outside with NORMAN.

A slight pause.

NORMAN is now working on the tyres.

Suddenly there is a rush of air. A door closes very suddenly.

MRS DODGE: (*Excited*) Wot 'appened?
NORMAN: (*Breathless and wildly excited*) I've done it!
               I've done it!

MRS DODGE: All right … All right, keep your shirt on!

NORMAN: I split the blinkin' tyre from one end of the wheel to the other!

MRS DODGE: Blimey, that's put an end to their outing an' no mistake.

The door bell rings.

NORMAN: Here he is … answer the door, Mrs Dodge.

MRS DODGE: O.K.

The door opens.

MAN: (*Pleasantly*) Good afternoon. I'm representing the Newhealth Insurance Company and I was wondering if …

MRS DODGE: Blimey – so am I. I'm just wondering if your blinkin' tyres is insured!

END OF EPISODE FIVE

EPISODE SIX

LUCY: Do listen to this, dear, it sounds most attractive. (*Reading*) "Paris, that colourful, effervescent city whose liveliness and friendly gaiety inspire the imagination of every visitor …"

ROBERT: (*A little wearily*) I thought you wanted to go to Lucerne?

LUCY: But we definitely decided against Italy because of the spaghetti.

ROBERT: Lucy … Lucerne is in Switzerland …and there is no spaghetti!!!!

LUCY: (*Rather hurt*) I'm sure there's no need to get excited, Robert. It's the sort of mistake anyone might make. After all, most foreigners do eat spaghetti – and it's no good saying they don't because Cousin Maude said …

ROBERT: Lucy, the fact that Cousin Maude once made a fleeting visit to Jersey on an August Bank Holiday is not sufficient reason for quoting her continental experiences at every conceivable opportunity! In fact, my love, keep Cousin Maude out of the conversation!!!!

LUCY: (*Meekly*) Very well, Robert … but Cousin Maude …

ROBERT: If you think Paris would be nice then we'll go to Paris. Personally I think it would be quite a good idea. I'd rather like Norman to see the Louvre.

LUCY: Do you think he's quite old enough for that sort of …

ROBERT: The Louvre, my dear! The Louvre!!!!

LUCY: Oh, yes, of course! How stupid of me … Yes, darling, that would be nice. Yes, I think we'll go to Paris. Of course, there is Le Touquet … and Ostend … and I suppose we might think of …

ROBERT: We might think of anything, dear … But we're going to Paris!!!!
LUCY: Cousin Maude thought of going to Paris one year but … (*She realises her mistake*) … but … but … she didn't.

ROBERT laughs.
FADE DOWN of laugh.

FADE IN NORMAN.

NORMAN: Crikey, I don't understand it … We've never gone abroad other years.
JANE: I should have thought you'd have wanted to have gone abroad.
NORMAN: Listen who's talking! You don't want to go any more than I do …
JANE: I know – but I've got a reason. If we go to Clacton, Tom can come down for weekends!
NORMAN: Yes – on his motorbike!
JANE: So that's it, is it!
NORMAN: Well, he said I could ride it, so there's no need to be funny!
JANE: (*Pointedly*) I wonder if Elsie's going to be at Clacton again this year?
NORMAN: (*Off hand*) I rather think she is! Matter of fact I had a letter from her the other day and …
JANE: Oh! Oh! So that's another reason you're not so keen on going abroad. That's why you won't wear your new suit until August … That's why your fancy handkerchiefs are …
NORMAN: Shut up, Jane!
JANE: (*Thoughtfully*) I wonder if there's still a chance of us going to Clacton, you never know they …

NORMAN:	Not a hope! Only last night Dad said he was pretty sure we'd be going to Paris or somewhere like that.
JANE:	Oh, dear! What a life!

The door opens.

MRS DODGE enters.

MRS DODGE:	'Ello, wot are you two up to?
NORMAN:	Nothing, Mrs Dodge.
MRS DODGE:	Well, that's a change I must say!
NORMAN:	(*Suddenly*) I say, Mrs Dodge, do be a sport and help us …
MRS DODGE:	Delighted – I'm sure! What's the trouble?
JANE:	The fact of the matter is, Mrs Dodge … Mother and Dad want us all to go to Paris for our holidays and Norman and I want to go to Clacton – You see Tom could come down for weekends and …
MRS DODGE:	Our young man can ride his motorbike in between times, I suppose! Mm – well, I don't see what I can do about it, I'm sure. Still I might have a pot at it. Is your old man very keen on the Continent …?
JANE:	Not really, Mrs Dodge … but he seems to think we are … it's all very awkward.
MRS DODGE:	Well, you two 'ad better 'op it for a bit an' let me think things over … Where there's a will there's relations …
JANE:	(*Laughing*) Righto, Mrs Dodge.

The door closes.

MRS DODGE busies herself with the tea things. She sings to herself.

The door opens.

ROBERT:	Hello, Mrs Dodge!
LUCY:	I thought you'd gone, Mrs Dodge.

MRS DODGE: Shan't be long on, mam.

We hear the rattle of the tea things.

MRS DODGE: 'Ear you're popping over to Paris for the 'olidays …

ROBERT: Yes, we thought it might be a change.

MRS DODGE: It'll be a change all right … 'Ope you're not taking the youngsters though …?

ROBERT: Why, of course we are!

MRS DODGE: (*Shocked*) What with all them there things going on …

ROBERT: (*Puzzled*) What things …?

MRS DODGE: Why, things like the Folies Bergere … and all them night places in Montmartre … and them dances and apaches and whatnots! Blimey – you won't half 'ave a basinful!

LUCY: We shall visit the Louvre and the … er … museums and perhaps a cinema or two … but certainly no night clubs!

MRS DODGE: Well – you know best I suppose! (*She is thinking fast*) Ah well – there won't be any 'oliday for me this year, that I do know.

LUCY: Why not, Mrs Dodge?

MRS DODGE: Oh, it's my old man …

ROBERT: Don't say he's got the sack again?

MRS DODGE: He hasn't got it yet but it's on the way. I told 'im not to have anything to do with the money when the blinkin' club first started.

ROBERT: What club?

MRS DODGE: An 'oliday club they formed at the works. Made our Ernie the treasurer they did.

ROBERT: Don't say he's mislaid some of the savings …?

MRS DODGE: I like the way you puts it I must say! Mislaid … I wish some of the others would

186

	be a little more careful in their choice o' words.
ROBERT:	But I say … isn't this rather serious, Mrs Dodge?
MRS DODGE:	Serious? I should think it blinkin' well is serious. Losing twenty quid ain't a laughing matter, you can take my word for it.
ROBERT:	Twenty pounds!
MRS DODGE:	(*Worried*) I don't know what we're going to do I'm sure. My 'ubby reckons he left it in a bus. He might 'ave left it anywhere – got a memory like a sieve.
ROBERT:	I say, this is serious, isn't it? If your husband was the treasurer he might be held responsible …
MRS DODGE:	If they sticks my old man in quod I don't know wot I'll do I'm sure. As for me! Blimey, I'll never be able to 'old me 'ead up again. You wouldn't get me staying in this neighbourhood, that I do know. (*She sighs*) Oh well, I'd better get on with me job … every minute counts.

The door closes.

LUCY:	Things look pretty bad for her, don't they?
ROBERT:	(*Thoughtfully*) Yes – Can't imagine the place without Mrs Dodge.
LUCY:	(*After a slight pause*) Robert …
ROBERT:	Yes …?
LUCY:	I suppose we couldn't lend her the money …?
ROBERT:	Well, we could but it'd mean goodbye to gay Paree. Probably have to go to Clacton again.

A pause.

LUCY:	Well – after all there's an … (*Speaking*
ROBERT:	Well – after all there's an … *at once*)
LUCY:	Go on …
ROBERT:	No, carry on, Lucy …
LUCY:	Well, I was going to say. There's an awfully nice pier at Clacton.
ROBERT:	And the bowling club! (*A pause*) Well, which is it to be … Mrs Dodge or Paris? … "Paris that colourful, effervescent city whose loveliness and friendly gaiety inspire the inspiration of every visitor …"
LUCY:	Well … perhaps after all, Robert, the book might be exaggerating, and you know what Mrs Dodge said …
ROBERT:	Very well, mother. That settles it. (*Suddenly*) Here's the children!

The door opens.

Enter JANE and NORMAN.

NORMAN:	Hello, Dad! We thought you were in the garden!
ROBERT:	Come in, Norman!
JANE:	What's the matter, Mummy, you both look as if …
LUCY:	Jane … I'm afraid you're going to be disappointed. You see your father and I have decided … Well, that is … well …
ROBERT:	The fact of the matter is – the Paris trip is off … We're all going to Clacton.
NORMAN:	(*Delighted*) Clac … Clacton!!!
JANE:	(*Thrilled*) We're not going to Paris!
LUCY:	No, dear – I'm afraid not. Next year perhaps!
ROBERT:	I'm sorry, children! Come along, Mother, we must have a word with Mrs Dodge!

The door closes.

JANE: I say, isn't it marvellous!

NORMAN: Whoopee! (*After a pause*) I wonder what
                 Mrs Dodge said to them …

JANE: Mrs Dodge …? What makes you think …?

NORMAN: Oh, it's Mrs Dodge all right … didn't you
                 hear Father say that …

The door opens.

Enter MRS DODGE.

MRS DODGE: Well, you two look a bit different I must
                 say! Blimey, just look at Norman!

JANE: Mrs Dodge … you've heard the news?

MRS DODGE: I've heard the news all right, dearie …

NORMAN: (*Almost in a whisper*) What happened?

MRS DODGE: I told 'em that my old man 'ad lost twenty
                 quid wot belonged to the works. Spun 'em a
                 yarn about 'im being the treasurer of the
                 'oliday funds. Proper upset 'em it did …
                 Your Pa is lending me the twenty quid to
                 put matters right – That's why you can't go
                 to Paris …

NORMAN: But – But what'll happen …?

MRS DODGE: Oh, don't worry, he'll get his twenty quid
                 back all right! As soon as you're all planted
                 at Clacton, I'll say the money's been found!

JANE: Then Mr Dodge didn't lose the twenty
                 pounds at all?

MRS DODGE: Not on your life! This year we're 'aving the
                 first proper holiday in thirty years!

NORMAN: Where are you going?

MRS DODGE: Where are we going? To that colourful
                 syrupofigs city whose liveliness an' friendly
                 gaiety inspire the imagination of every
                 visitor … That's where we're going, my lad.
                 PARIS!

END OF EPISODE SIX

www.ingramcontent.com/pod-product-compliance
Lightning Source LLC
Chambersburg PA
CBHW020324260626
47156CB00004B/1367